Baby, Maybe

Lyssa Layne

The characters and events in this book are fictitious. Any similarity to real persons, living or dead, places, or events is coincidental and not intended by the author.

If you purchase this book without a cover you should be aware that this book may have been stolen property and reported as "unsold and destroyed" to the publisher. In such case the author has not received any payment for this "stripped book."

Baby, Maybe
Copyright © 2017 Lyssa Layne
All rights reserved.

This book, or parts thereof, may not be reproduced in any form without permission. The copying, scanning, uploading, and distribution of this book via the internet or via any other means without the permission of the publisher is illegal and punishable by law. Please purchase only authorized electronic or print editions, and do not participate in or encourage piracy of copyrighted materials. Your support of the author's rights is appreciated.

DEDICATION

Dedicated to the real life Julie and Shawn, an amazing couple who are the true meaning of #relationshipgoals

I adore our friendship but hate how our paths crossed. #infertilitysucks #1in8

ACKNOWLEDGEMENTS

When I signed up to be part of the Luck of the Draw box set, I had no idea what I'd planned on writing. It was through a late night conversation with Alison Foster that this idea came to me! Once I figured it out, thanks to Alison, I knew it was time for me to write the story that had been begging to come out ever since I wrote my first book. I always intended to write this story about Julie and Shawn but ended up using knowledge from both her journey to parenthood and my own. In a complete bout of randomness, Julie and I crossed paths when I had just become pregnant with AR. The moment I met her husband, Shawn, I loved him! He is such a genuine, caring man that adores Julie. I'll always remember Julie coming to visit me while I was on maternity leave so she could meet AR. I know how difficult that was for her but it just proves what an amazing friend that she is. These two people are a one-of-a-kind couple and I'm grateful to call them my friends. While I loved writing about you two, it was a bit creepy to stalk your Facebook so I could have accurate descriptions of you both!

To those of you that have experienced infertility, this story will hit home on so many levels. It's raw, it's real, it's ugly, but it was the story of my life for almost two years. The sad thing is that two years is short in the infertility world. Beautiful, amazing people like Julie and Shawn struggle for so much longer and it doesn't get easier as the years go on. As I wrote this story, I was worried that the main character may seem a little "woe is me" but I wanted this story to be real and her emotions are exactly what almost every woman struggling to get pregnant feels. For those of you that haven't experienced it, I hope you never do except in this story. If you know someone that is, be a friend, let them vent, and don't tell them to "just relax." To those of you that are my sisters in infertility, you are amazing, only those of us strong enough to survive are chosen for this path.

Now, after the story, there's always the behind the scenes that makes the magic of a story come to life. A huge shoutout and show of gratitude to Rebecca Austin and Dawn Brock for beta reading and giving me your honest feedback, Melissa Keir for your formatting skills, Barb Piper for proofreading, Katie Beach of Katie Beach Photography for the gorgeous photo of my daughter and I on the cover, and to Amanda Walker for making a memory into a cover. To my Lovers of Lyssa Layne, I will always be grateful for your continued support and love.

To Dr. Sarah Keller, Dr. Valerie Ratts, and Dr. Kenan Omurtag, thank you for my beautiful daughter and for enduring all of my craziness!

PROLOGUE

"I want a divorce."

His sentence echoes through my mind on repeat with no pause button to push. He uttered those words five months ago but it's still as clear as the first time he spoke them. It's not that I disagree with ending our marriage, it was over almost before it began. I was never a priority, being outranked by his friends, hunting, paintball, or anything else that wasn't me. We'd been living separate lives long before he spoke those four words that changed our entire lives. It was like we were distant roommates that were forced to spend holidays together.

"Mommy! Turn up the radio, it's Meghan Trainor!" The curly haired blonde three-year-old shouts at me from the backseat.

I smile and do as she dictated, not taking the time to remind her to use "please." The Goldilocks behind me is the reason I'm distraught over my marriage ending. She's the reason I'd planned on sucking it up for the next fifteen years so that I never lost a single second with her. I fought to get pregnant with her and I sure as hell am going to fight to keep her as much as possible.

"Oh, Mommy, look! It's your favorite tree!"

To the right is a giant evergreen lit up with colorful strands of Christmas lights. 'Tis the season for Christmas decorations and a welcomed distraction from the real world that haunts me every day. Aside from kissing my girl goodnight, this is one of the other highlights of my days lately. We drive down our street before the sun is up, heading to the babysitter's house, and we call out to each other which lights are our favorite. Listening to her voice squeak with excitement always brings a smile to my face and I wish we could drive around all day looking at Christmas lights.

Her favorite, yet highly inappropriate, Meghan Trainor song ends and the DJ begins to explain a contest they're running where a lucky listener could win $50,000. I'm only half listening because I'm not lucky, then again, apparently there's a lot of things I'm not. I'm not a good wife. I'm not a good listener. I'm not a good lover. I'm not, I'm not, I'm not, but I really am. Personally, I think I'm an awesome person. I'm funny, compassionate, caring, giving... just not to him and it's his words that mean more to me than they should. It's his words that make me feel like a failure, that make me wonder how I have a single friend in the entire world.

"Hey, Mommy?"

I glance in the rearview mirror. "Yes, baby?"

"I love you."

Tears well in my eyes. I must be doing something right to get that. Not wanting to let my daughter see me cry, I force a smile to my face. It's time to stop thinking about what I'm not. I need positivity in my life. I need something to make me feel good about myself. I need to spread the love because everyone has a cross to carry.

"I love you, too, baby."

The moment is over as she shouts about three more houses we're passing. The people inside those houses covered with bright lights have no idea how much they've impacted our lives or the number of smiles they've created.

BABY, MAYBE

It's time to pay it forward, it's time to pimp some positivity.

CHAPTER 1

"Come on, Shawn, my temperature is spot on and my cervical mucus is an indicator that I'm ovulating!" I shout, way too excited than anyone should ever be when they're yelling about mucus.

My husband, the dark skinned, sexy man that he is appears in the doorway wearing a pair of red and black plaid, flannel pajama pants and a white t-shirt. Never mind that I know there's a hole in the crotch of the pants or that there's an ice cream stain on his shirt, and I'm really praying that he's brushed his teeth already, because I know my man is sexy... yes, so sexy... and hot... *Keep thinking that, Julie, keep thinking that!*

"I have to get ready for work," he comments, making no effort to even entertain a quickie before breakfast.

I lean up on my elbows, shaking my blonde locks over the pillow, trying to entice him to join me in bed. "Come on, Shawn, don't you want a little lovin' before work?" I ask, using my most seductive voice, and even I cringe at how ridiculous I sound.

Shawn flips on the overhead light, blinding me before I can cover my eyes. "Yeah, Jules, I would love to *make love* with my wife, not *have sex* because her temperature is right and her cervical mucus is thick."

He shakes his head and pulls off his shirt as he stands in front of our closet, looking for an outfit for the day. I jump out of bed and run up behind him, pressing my bare chest flush against his back and sliding my hands over the front of his flannel pants.

"Then let's make love, baby… right now." I try to hide the urgency in my voice but Shawn knows it's a limited window of when I'm ovulating and everything must be lined up perfectly.

Shawn's large hands move over mine and hope surges through me that he's reconsidering my offer. If we don't have sex this morning, it'll be a whole month before we can try to get pregnant again. In the big scheme of things, what's another month, right? Well, after ten years of trying to get pregnant, another month is a lifetime away.

Without warning, Shawn pushes my hands off him and turns around to face me. His eyes travel up and down my naked body. His body language is making this whole situation too wishy washy for me to know whether I should continue to pursue or step back. He usually always comes around, no pun intended.

Shaking his head, my husband lets out a long sigh. "I want you, Julie, I always do. Every time I see you naked, I want nothing more than to make love to you, but when you proposition me with words like temperature and mucus, it kills my libido faster than having my mom walk in on you giving me a blowjob."

Tears sting my eyes at his honesty. I bite my bottom lip, trying not to cry until he throws in that horrible memory from the first year we were married and then I let out a small laugh.

"I want a baby just as much as you do and I know we've spent a lot of years trying—"

"Ten," I whisper, "Ten years we've been trying to get pregnant. A decade. We could have a middle—"

Shawn grabs my shoulders, squeezing them tightly and

applying just enough pressure to bring my nerves down a notch. "Okay, ten years we've been trying, but it's the holidays, Jules. Let's not put all the pressure on us for this month. Let's just enjoy our holiday parties, have a relaxing Christmas, get drunk on New Year's, and then start fresh on the babymaking next year?"

The words "next year" unleash the tears and they fall faster than Niagara Falls. I push my hands against his chest, shrugging off his hold on my arms, and take a step back. "Next year? *Next year?* Shawn, do you even want a baby? You know that if you drink on New Year's that we have to wait at least a month for your sperm to be even viable to possibly get pregnant? You know the success rate for women drops significantly after thirty-five and I'll be thirty-five in September? We might as well not even—"

Shawn taps his index finger on the side of my head. "Can you hear yourself, Julie? You're making yourself crazy! You've twisted all these facts that we've heard over the years."

Leaning over, I pick up his stained t-shirt he just discarded and pull it on, crossing my arms over the mess he left behind. "I am *not* crazy, Shawn. I'm just dedicated." More tears fall because I know I'd make a great mother, just look how hard I'm trying to get pregnant and imagine what I'd do for that baby once the little one was actually here.

My husband, the man who is normally a giant teddy bear, lets out a loud sigh and crosses his arms, the ones I normally love to be held with. He shakes his head when he begins to speak in his kind, gentle tone that's talked me off proverbial bridges in the past. "It's not that I don't want to have a child with you, Julie. It's just that I'm realistic. We've tried for ten years, a decade, to get pregnant almost every, single month and it hasn't happened. I can't even remember how many IUIs we've done, two IVFS, and it hasn't happened yet. I'm not trying to be an asshole but the deck is stacked against us to get pregnant on our own.

Maybe if we stop worrying about it and enjoy life until we can afford another IVF and it'll work out next time?"

My sad tears are replaced with angry ones as rage boils through my veins. I try to mimic his tone, sounding as calm as I can, but speaking through clenched teeth. "Don't worry? Enjoy life? You know I hate when people tell us that. *'Don't worry, it'll happen.' 'Maybe you're too stressed, that's why you can't get pregnant.' 'You should really enjoy life without kids now because you won't have a life when you do.'* It's so insensitive, Shawn! I expect those kinds of comments from strangers or your mother, but not from you!"

Shawn rolls his eyes, throwing up his hands and I know I went too far with the mother comment.

"Unlike you, I wasn't trying to be insensitive. I'm trying to be the realistic one here and save our marriage before a kid we don't even have yet drives us apart."

He grabs a shirt off a hanger and a pair of pants then exits the room without even looking at me. His words sting like a slap across the face, not that I would know what the feels like, but I can imagine. Shawn is the most kind, patient, loving man in the entire world and he's right, I'm going to drive him away with all my craziness of trying to get pregnant. He's been by my side for ten years during our journey and I've taken for granted that he'll always be in that same spot, maybe this is his hint that he may not always be. Either way, I need to get myself together before I end up not only childless but an old maid, too.

CHAPTER 2

My eyes are fixated on the perfectly round bump in front of me. I desperately want to reach out and touch it but being that I don't know anything more than Molly's name from her Walmart name tag, I keep my hands to myself and let my mind wander. My thoughts float away to a time where I'll be the one with the round belly and everyone will want to touch it. Of course, I'll act completely annoyed when people ask if they can like all pregnant women do but deep down, I'll be elated because it will mean that I have a teeny, tiny baby growing inside me.

"You're an adorable pregnant woman. When are you due?" I ask casually, trying not to stare as I hand Molly cash for the ovulation strips I'm purchasing, the strips that I promised Shawn I wouldn't buy after our conversation this morning. I couldn't help it that my mind was on autopilot as I navigated the aisles of Walmart and I headed straight to that section out of habit. By the time I realized what I was buying, there was already a line behind me and it was too late to abort mission.

"Ugh, please don't say that! I feel so disgusting and huge!" Molly exclaims.

My face flushes red, unaware that there were certain phrases I wasn't supposed to say to pregnant women. I'm all too aware of the phrases *not* to say to women who aren't pregnant. "When are you and Shawn going to have kids?" "You're not getting any younger, Julie." And then there's the shock and awe when I tell people that we've been married for over ten years and don't have any kids. I sigh, feeling sorry for myself like most days.

"Sorry," I mumble. "Pregnancy is just such a beautiful thing, it's hard not to admire when a woman is carrying a human life."

Molly lets out a hoot and throws her hair back as she laughs. "Not when it's your third time around, then it's just old news. I swear my body will never be normal again."

I feel my jaw get heavy, ready to drop at the news that this is Molly's third time to be pregnant. The blonde barely looks like she's out of high school, much less the soon to be mother of three children.

"Ho-how old are you?"

Molly rolls her brown eyes. "You going to be all judgy because I'm not even legal to drink alcohol yet?"

My stomach sinks and tears sting my eyes. Why? Why her and not me? What have I done to be punished like this? I graduated from high school with honors, waited until I was nineteen to lose my virginity, graduated college a year early magna cum laude, and have been a contributing member of society ever since. Shawn and I didn't even move in together until we got engaged, we're both working middle class Americans yet for whatever reason, we've been chosen as the 'lucky' ones to be barren.

I thrust my money at Molly, not even waiting for my change as I collect my ovulation strips and run out of the store. My waterworks begin the second the greeter tells me to have a nice day and by the time I reach my vehicle, I'm a blubbering mess, both irritated at Molly's third pregnancy and myself for getting upset with her. I know first-hand that infertility doesn't discriminate, it doesn't care how much money you make or where you're from. I know better than to "be all judgy" as Molly would say.

Leaning forward, I set my head on the steering wheel, trying to get ahold of myself, but only scaring the bejeezus out of me when I hit the horn instead. My heart races, tears still falling down my cheeks, and I can't do anything but laugh. This is my life. How did it get to this point? Tilting my head back against the seat, I sigh, because I allowed it to get to this point. I let infertility take over me. Every day I wake up, I should feel blessed to be alive but instead, I feel cursed to not be pregnant. I don't even know how to live life any more without letting infertility take over. No wonder Shawn is so upset with me.

Out of nowhere, I suddenly feel like I might vomit when the thought that Shawn probably should've left me years ago sprints through my mind. The car keys are still in my lap but I grip the steering wheel tightly, afraid I might lose control of the car just like I have with my life. My knuckles white, I take a deep breath and make a vow to myself, right here in the middle of this Walmart parking lot with a pregnant twenty-year-old Molly inside as my witness, well at least in my mind she is. I, Julie Hampton, do solemnly swear… wait, am I marrying myself or what? Shaking my head, I loosen my grip on the steering wheel. Moving forward, I'm going to try to not let infertility lead my life. I'm going to enjoy the time that I have with Shawn before the little pitter patter of baby feet fill our house… and it will because I have to be a mother, right? I sigh because I don't know what I'll do if I never experience what it's like to have a child of my own.

CHAPTER 3

Three stores later and I finally find myself in my kitchen wearing nothing but a black satin chemise. I've cranked up the heat since I'm waltzing around, cooking dinner in next to nothing. I've also lit every candle in our house and scattered them throughout the dining room. I can confidently say I have set the ambiance for when Shawn arrives home but from pumpkin spice to pineapple mango, the mix of the candle scents are making me a bit nauseous.

Opening a drawer, I dig for our wine opener that I haven't used in ages. At one point, it was used on at least a monthly basis to help me cope with that unwelcome womanly visitor that let me know I was yet again without child. Digging through pot holders and boxes of toothpicks, I finally find the opener and waste no time getting the bottle of moscato open. Pouring a small sampling into a dusty wine glass that I just wiped down, I bring the cup to my lips and inhale. *Mmm...* the wine fizzes as it swirls in the glass and the luscious smell tickles my nose. Opening my mouth, I let the sweet moscato touch my taste buds and I let out a small moan as I enjoy my first sip of wine in years. Alcohol and apparently real, passionate sex with my husband are two things I've been depriving myself of since we started trying to conceive but that all changes tonight.

Quickly, I gulp down the rest of my wine and pour myself another. Turning up my iPod, I turn my attention back to the Italian fest I'm preparing while singing along with the Chainsmokers. I should clarify that when I say Italian feast I mean I'm boiling noodles and adding a can of Prego spaghetti sauce. I pause as I stare at the label of the spaghetti sauce, recalling a pregnancy announcement from my friend Meg… 'Mego is Prego' she posted as the caption when she changed her social media picture to a jar of Prego. Refilling my glass of wine, I swallow down another big gulp, forcing myself to not think about all the pregnancy announcements I'd planned over the years.

"Jules, you home?" Shawn calls out, throwing the mail on the counter.

The overhead kitchen light flips on and I throw my arm over my face, trying to keep from my retinas being blinded by the sudden light. Blinking, I realize how ridiculous I must look with my arm contorted over my head while I'm wearing this silly lingerie. Wishing I could rewind time to when this stupid idea crossed my mind, I hear a low whistle.

"Damn, baby, you look hot," Shawn says, pulling my arm away from my face and resting his hands on my hips.

I bite my bottom lip, still feeling foolish as I stand in the middle of our kitchen with my butt cheeks hanging out. Speaking of butt cheeks, my husband squeezes them as his head dips to my ear and he nibbles on them. Butterflies bat their wings in my stomach and for the first time since I read that first negative pregnancy test, I'm excited for sex, not because I might get pregnant but because my husband is going to tease and tempt and tickle my every last desire.

"So, what's the special occasion?" Shawn whispers in my ear.

Without notice, he maneuvers his hands and sweeps me into his arms, walking us toward the bedroom. Squealing with surprise, I link my hands around his neck as Shawn continues teasing my ear with his teeth. I sigh and tilt my head back, remembering the days when we were carefree and there wasn't so much pressure on us to have a baby. The pressure is never ending and it's not just from each other but from our families, co-workers, friends, church members. It's like a question with no answer that is being asked on repeat. Tears burn my eyes as I want to cry just thinking about how many times we've been asked when we're going to have kids but luckily, Shawn repeats his question.

"Hmm, babe, what brought out the kinky lingerie tonight?"

Gently, he sets me on the bed as I laugh. Smiling, I reach out and touch his cheek lightly as I brush my lips against his. This man is so good to me, he treats me like a princess, and he'd make a great fath—

"You were right this morning. I'm going crazy over all this babymaking and I'm missing out on this wonderful life right in front of me. I wanted to give you one night in the bedroom without the stress of what the outcome could be."

Shawn kisses my forehead and shakes his head. "You aren't crazy, baby, you're determined. It's why I fell in love with you and it's why I fall even deeper in love with you every day."

My heart melts at his sincerity and I run my hand down his chest. "Whatever I am, crazy or determined or whatever, I want to take a break from all the babymaking. No more ovulation strips or temperature checks or thickness of my cervical mucus, let's spend the holidays and the new year just enjoying each other without the pressure of getting pregnant."

Shawn's lips grow into a giant grin and he nods. "I like that idea…"

He trails off and I end up yelping again as his hand parts my legs and takes me by surprise one more time. I close my eyes, enjoying the touch of my husband's fingers moving over my panties and across the silk material covering my breasts. My face begins to flush as my body grows stronger and stronger in desire to feel my husband in every way possible. As my body heats up, I squeeze my eyes tighter and it's almost as though I'm dreaming that I'm so hot the smoke alarm is going off.

"Shit," Shawn mutters and I open my eyes, realizing that my dream is really a reality as the smoke alarm screams loudly from downstairs. Shawn pulls his hands away from me and as much as I don't want our house to burn down, I also don't want to lose his touch. He's already racing down the stairs before I get a chance to beg him to stay. Reluctantly, I sit up and follow him downstairs where the kitchen is filled with smoke.

"Shawn!" I call out in a panic, the actuality of the situation setting in. Unable to see or hear him right away, my heart races into a panic until the beeping comes to a halt. Knowing he's okay somewhere in this cloud of smoke, my heart rate begins to slow and I wait for Shawn to appear. A chilly breeze hits me like a brick wall and I immediately begin to shiver since I'm still wearing next to nothing with damp underwear on. Through the smoke, I hear the familiar sound of Shawn's laughter and I rest a little easier.

"I think this pan is toast," Shawn says and I hear a loud thud as he drops it into the trash can. "Guess we both got distracted and forgot about the stove being on."

Waving my hands, I clear my way to where Shawn is standing next to the door that leads out to the garage. He opens his arms when he sees me and I snuggle up to him in an effort to stay warm, and also in relief that I didn't burn the house down. Inhaling deeply, Shawn's thick, musky cologne tickles my nose and immediately, my libido jumps back into full force.

Sliding my arms around his neck, I kiss his chin and whisper, "Let's go back to the bedroom…"

I take a step back but quickly notice that Shawn isn't moving. Reaching around me, he picks up my Walmart bag and lets go of me. He opens the sack and pulls out the ovulation strips, holding them up. With his other hand, he grabs the receipt and skims it then shakes his head.

"What the hell, Julie? What was all that talk earlier about taking a break? Not worrying about getting pregnant? What was tonight? One of your crazy schemes to get me to 'relax' in hopes that you'll get knocked up?" He pauses although I know he wants to say more, probably so much more, but he can control his emotions much better than I can. My husband holds up his hands, shaking his head as he walks backward toward the door. "I'm your husband, Julie. I'm the one person in this entire world that you're supposed to be totally honest with and never lie to. I'm done, I can't do this."

My heart drops to the bottom of my stomach and I lunge after him, desperate to not let him walk away. "Shawn, no! Don't go, don't say that. I'm sorry, I'm so sorry! I didn't get those strips for tonight… I… I don't even know why I bought them. Don't leave me, Shawn, don't go!" Tears stream down my face and I desperately beg my husband to stay. It's one thing to never have children but I know I'd never survive a life without Shawn.

Shawn pauses, putting his hand behind my head and pulling me to him so he can kiss my forehead. "I'm not leaving you, Julie, but I need to think, I need to get away from here tonight."

I shake my head, a giant lump in my throat, unable to speak again and beg him one more time to stay. I don't have to say anything though, my husband knows what I'm thinking.

"I love you and I'll be back. I just need some fresh air to clear my mind. You're my girl, Julie, but we've got to get on the same page." With a light kiss to my forehead, my husband, the love of my life walks out the door and I'm so afraid he's not coming back. I'm going to lose my husband if I don't get this baby fever out of my mind and pronto.

CHAPTER 4

It's been almost twenty-four hours since I've seen Shawn and to say I'm freaking out would be the understatement of the year. Granted, we've texted throughout the day but until I see him in person and know that he's coming home, I won't relax. From the moment he walked out the door, I've made a list of what I can do to curb my desire to get pregnant and push the thought of all our fertility issues aside. I was up until midnight packing away every book about fertility or pregnancy and anything else that was related to babymaking, I even deleted the ovulation apps on my phone. After that, I still couldn't sleep so I spent the early morning hours of today scrubbing our house from top to bottom. With only the kitchen left, I'm tidying up the counter as I watch the minutes tick by, hoping Shawn will walk in the door any second.

I pick up the mail he set on the counter last night when I surprised him with wearing next to nothing when he walked in the door. Despite feeling silly, I smile as I recall the surprise and excitement on his face when he saw me. Mindlessly, I thumb through the Christmas cards, all probably with pictures of our friends and families' adorable children, my mind wandering back a few years ago when we first started trying to conceive, or TTC, and I was so sure that we'd be using our Christmas cards to announce our own pregnancy that year. I start to think about the exact wording I'd planned on using but then I realize that I'm doing it. I'm letting the whole TTC issue take over me and I don't even realize it.

Snapping out of my trance, a card in the pile catches my attention. It isn't the traditional holiday card, it's not even in an envelope. It's a piece of paper someone printed off their home computer and folded in half. On the outside, it simply says, "Thanks for lighting up our holidays." When I open the paper, the message hand-printed on the inside brings tears to my eyes.

"Happy holidays! We don't know you and you don't know us but I wanted to thank you for lighting up my daughter and my holiday season. We've been going through a rough patch lately but every morning when we drive by your house, my daughter calls out to me with so much joy and excitement about your Christmas lights that it gives me a slight escape from my day to day issues. So for that, I thank you and we wish you happy holidays. May luck be on your side!"

Taped on the top half of the card is a scratch-off lottery ticket. Tears cloud my eyes and one plops in the middle of the stranger's handwriting, smearing her words slightly. Quickly, I grab the kitchen towel and dab it, not wanting to ruin her sentiment. I drop the note on the counter, too afraid that my tears will do more harm to the letter. I slide down the counter, dropping to my backside and leaning my arms on my legs as I cradle my head. In the disappointment of big, fat, negative pregnancy tests, month after month, I forgot what life was like outside of my own little bubble. I forgot that other people hurt for their own reasons. Here, this beautiful stranger, took a few minutes out of her day to help brighten mine and all because we just decorated the house for the holidays.

"Jules! Are you okay?"

Glancing up, I see Shawn close the door and take a few quick steps to me, dropping to his knees. He pulls me against his chest and my sobs unleash, every emotion from fear of losing him to disappointment of not being pregnant to not feeling like we deserve this stranger's lottery ticket hits me like a racecar running into a brick wall. The comfort of my husband's strong arms and safety of being in his grasp helps me gain control of my meltdown as I hold on to him tightly.

"I'm sorry about everything, Shawn. I don't want a baby if it means losing you. I promise I'll change and I—"

"Whoa, whoa, whoa, babe." Shawn leans back, lifting my chin up so I have to look at him. "I never said it was a baby or me. All I'm saying is that we need a timeout. *You* need to enjoy life, Julie, stop letting this whole babymaking thing control you."

I nod, sniffling as I do.

Shawn kisses my nose. "I'm not leaving you now or later, babe. You're stuck with me."

My lips twitch into a smile and I nod. "Promise?"

Shawn's giant smile that I love so much, the one that reaches his eyes and brightens the whole room appears. "Promise."

Kissing me lightly, he pulls away slowly and stands up, taking my hand and pulling me up with him. I wrap my arms around his neck, taking a few seconds to admire this man of mine before I push up on my tippy toes and lightly touch my lips to his. Just like the first time we kissed, butterflies dance in my stomach and I'm comforted by the thought that we'll be okay, baby or not, we're going to be just fine. The kiss ends and Shawn's grin gets even bigger.

"What do you say we pick up where we left off last night?"

I smile. "That sounds like a plan. Why don't you head upstairs and I'll be up in a minute?"

My sexy, dark skinned man walks backward as he exits

the room, pulling his shirt over his head in the most unattractive way that turns me on more than anything Channing Tatum could ever do. Laughing at his antics, I wait until he's out of the room then pick up the stranger's card again. Gently, I pull off the lottery ticket and dig through my purse for a penny to scratch it off. Rubbing off one number at a time, I try to tell myself that I'm not as bad as I feel like I am. Maybe I should take a hint from this stranger to do more good on purpose for other people, lift them up like she's done for me.

All the numbers are uncovered and I scan the ticket to see if I won anything. After a quick double take, my breathing pauses and my entire body goes numb, like a million needles being stuck into my body. It takes a second for my brain to remind myself to breathe and immediately I start screaming for Shawn. It only takes twice as long for him to appear in the kitchen wearing nothing but his birthday suit and a concerned look on his face.

"What is it? What's wrong? Is there a spider?" Shawn's eyes dart around the room, looking for whatever danger there could be based off my screaming.

I thrust my arm out in his direction, holding the ticket for him to take. "Did we win?"

His eyebrows slant into a deep V and he shakes his head. "Win what? What is this? Where did it come—" He interrupts himself as he reads the ticket then looks up at me. "Is this for real?"

Slowly, still in a daze, I nod. "I... I think so. It was in this card you carried in last night."

Shawn takes the folded piece of paper and reads through it. "Don't get your hopes up, Jules. This could be a cruel joke. Let's run up to the gas station and have them scan it, see if it's real."

Before I can answer, Shawn is grabbing his keys, his hand on the doorknob. I clear my throat loud enough for him to turn around. When he turns to face me, he lifts his eyebrows to ask "what?"

With a smirk on my face, I nod in his direction. "Um... I think you might be forgetting something."

Shawn glances down at his naked body and laughs. "I guess what they say is true... money changes you."

Laughing, I walk across the room to him and throw my arms around his neck. "I love you, Shawn Hampton."

He laughs and kisses me passionately. "You're just saying that because we may have just won fifty-thousand dollars."

Rolling my eyes, I take the ticket from him and set it on the counter. "Nah, I'm saying that because you just walked in here wearing nothing but the outfit you were born in," I say as I playfully swat him on the backside. In one swift movement, my husband sweeps me into his arms as I let out a loud shrill as he carries me to the kitchen table.

"Money can wait..." he says, kissing me beneath my ear and sending bolts of electricity throughout my body, "I want my wife, right here, right now."

Smiling, I close my eyes as Shawn tugs off my pants. He's right, I need to live life. We need to have fun and *oh!* Mmhmm... this is definitely fun!

CHAPTER 5

The lemonade stands whirrs in the corner, circulating the yellow liquid and making me think of what the inside of my bladder looks like. I grip Shawn's hand tighter as I feel like I might be getting high from the strong aroma of marijuana permeating from the man standing in line in front of us. The flashing 'open' sign blinks a few feet away in the front window of the gas station and I realize I haven't been in a gas station past midnight since I was in college.

Shawn smiles down at me and squeezes my hand. My apprehension dissipates, comforted by the man at my side. My mouth quickly jumps into a grin, remembering why we're late... two orgasms later. It doesn't matter if this lottery ticket is real or not, I already won the lottery the day I met Shawn.

The stoner, I mean the overly medicated old man, stumbles out of the store and Shawn steps up to the counter. I follow behind him, still holding his hand as he sets the ticket on the counter. My husband clears his throat and in a very matter-of-fact voice, he states, "Good evening, sir. I believe we might have a winner on our hands."

BABY, MAYBE

The clerk flips his long, blond hair out of his eyes, not even bothering to look up at us. Surfer Boy, who might be even more blitzed than the old man that just left, takes the ticket off the counter, and I swear he's moving in slow motion. In the time it takes him to walk five steps to the opposite end of his work space, I could have guzzled down a Big Gulp and already gotten a refill. He scans the ticket and a long beep sounds. Then the single beep turns into a string of multiple ones and Shawn and I look at each other, tightening our grips on each other's hand.

"Wh-what's that mean?" I ask, trying not to get my hopes up.

Surfer Boy looks up, flipping his hair out of his face again. "Means you won."

"We-we won? How much?" My voice goes up an octave by the time I get the questions out.

The clerk, obviously irritated by us asking him to do his job, lets out a long sigh and looks back at the machine. "Five hundred."

"Oh," I mutter, disappointed that it wasn't what I'd been expecting.

Taking me by surprise, Shawn's thick hands grab my waist and he lifts me in the air as he lets out a loud whoop. "Five hundred bucks, baby! Five hundred! Think about what we could do with five hundred dollars, how lucky are we!

I laugh, knowing he's right. It's five hundred dollars more than we had before. I wrap my arms around his neck, kissing him passionately, trying to return the same excitement he's displaying. This is what he meant about living life, being excited about the little things, five hundred little things to be exact.

"Let's go away. A weekend trip to Cooperstown?"

Shawn's eyes go wide, no fake excitement now. "Like to the Baseball Hall of Fame?"

I nod, kissing the end of his nose. "Yep, Baseball Hall of Fame and all things baseball."

"But you hate baseball," he says, making an official statement that is one-hundred-percent true.

Laughing, I shrug. "You're right, I do, but I love you."

"Good god, Julie Hampton, I fall more and more in love with you every day." He picks me up, spinning me in a circle, narrowly missing the Cheeto rack.

Peace. Yesterday's fight is pushed out of my mind and I'm at peace again that everything will be okay. Shawn is my prince, he is my forever, even if it is just the two of us. He wants to know how lucky we are and all I can think is how lucky I am to have him.

Surfer Boy meanders back to the counter in front of us, handing Shawn the ticket. "Hey, man, I was wrong about what you won."

My stomach drops, hoping he doesn't say it was only fifty dollars and not five hundred. I don't want to let Shawn down again, like I do month after month when we get that BFN. My mind is calculating how much we have in our secret savings account, trying to figure out if we can spare $500 so we can still take that trip.

"Yeah, I was off a zero. It's actually fifty grand." Surfer Boy takes a seat on his stool then looks up and shrugs his shoulders. "My bad."

I turn to look at Shawn, my strong, confident husband, who is standing as still as a statue with his mouth gaping open. I tug on his hand and he slowly turns to me. In an instant, he shrieks like a little girl. Immediately, I cover my ears and begin laughing uncontrollably as Shawn picks me up again. Throwing caution to the wind, he spins us in a circle, knocking over the entire rack of Cheetos. Then the first thing my husband says after winning fifty thousand dollars is, "We'll take all of those!"

CHAPTER 6

Lying in bed, my chest heaves up and down as I try to catch my breath. It's amazing how in less than twenty-four hours, Shawn and I went from the lowest of lows in our marriage to the highest of highs. After days, months, years of planned intercourse, we've had complete and total spontaneous sex twice in a matter of hours. If only his sperm would fertilize one of my eggs, it would be the icing on the cake.

"Can you believe we just won fifty thousand dollars?" Shawn asks as he pops open a bag of Cheetos and the smell of powdered cheese fills the air.

"You're sure that was really the lottery commission that you called?" Having caught my breath, I roll over, laying half my body on Shawn's chest. Lazily, I drag my finger up and down his abdomen, loving the contrast of my pale skin against his dark.

"For the fifty thousandth time, I'm sure." He pauses and does this half-chuckle noise he makes when he's pleased with himself. "Did you see what I did there? Fifty-thousandth time?"

My head bounces up and down as he starts to laugh harder and I join him. "Yes, goofball, I see what you did."

Sitting up, I straddle my husband, his manhood touching the inside of my thigh. "You better not get your Cheeto fingers all over the bed."

Shawn's brown eyes light up with mischief. "Honey, we can get Cheeto mess all over the bed because we can buy a new one. And then when I get my Cheeto fingers all over that, we'll buy ANOTHER new one. You know why?"

Rolling my eyes, I shake my head. "We are not wasting all of our money on Cheetos and new beds."

He reaches out, his index finger covered in orange Cheeto dust, and drags it between my breasts. "Too late on the Cheeto thing, we have another fifty thousand bags downstairs."

His finger rolls over my nipple, tweaking it and leaving Cheeto residue on my skin. Shawn replaces his finger with his mouth, sucking off the mess he's left behind. I tilt my head back, closing my eyes and enjoying the warmth of his mouth of my skin. Rubbing my hand over his bald scalp, I sigh, remembering a simpler time in our relationship and how far we'd gotten away from this kind of intimacy. I lean my head up and kiss the top of his head.

"I love you, Shawn Hampton," I whisper.

Shawn looks up, his permanent smile still tickling his lips. "I love you, too, baby." He shakes his head. "I still can't believe it, we won fifty thousand *dollars!*"

He shakes his head with a laugh and lies back on the bed. Sitting on his thighs, I run my hands over his stomach and nod. "It's crazy, isn't it? How lucky are we?"

Shawn folds his arms behind his head, his grin still hanging there and I think this might be his new look. "Real lucky, baby, but I already knew I was. I mean, you are my wife after all."

Still, after all these years together, my cheeks tinge red from his compliment. "I feel the same way."

He shakes his head. "What are we going to do with the money? I don't want to wind up as one of those crazy stories on the True Life channel... 'lottery winners who lost it all.'"

I roll my eyes and laugh at him. Shrugging, I bite my tongue, knowing what I want to suggest but too afraid it might ruin the moment. He knows how much a cycle of IVF costs and he knows what fifty grand could afford us in fertility treatments but I don't say a word.

"Maybe we should play MASH to decide," I suggest, referring to the middle school game I used to play with my friends.

"MASH?"

"Yeah, you know... mansion, apartment, shack, house?" I quirk my eyebrow, appalled that my husband doesn't know what MASH is.

"You have completely lost me." Shawn shakes his head, giving me the same look and making me feel like I'm looking into a mirror.

Letting out an exasperated sigh, I roll my eyes. "It's a game we used to play in middle school to predict your future. You wrote MASH at the top of the page which stood for mansion, apartment, shack, or house. Then you'd pick story categories-potential husbands, number of kids, their names, your job. The person in charge of your story would draw a spiral to determine the 'magic number.' They'd count each of the category options until they reached the magic number then they'd continue around the page, skipping over the marked off options. Then they'd circle the final option in each category and viola, your life was written for you!"

Shawn shakes his head laughing. "One, why would you think I would have every played that game? And two, any of your stories come true?"

My cheeks redden and I shrug. "Well... no but if I'd known you in middle school, you would've been my only choice for husband."

He smiles, running his finger down my cheek. "Fair enough. Well, short of relying on a middle school game to predict our future, I was thinking, if you're still good with

Cooperstown, we could go on another trip of your choice." He watches my fingers walk across his chest. "Jamaica, Australia, Maine..."

Wow, he picked three great locations that he knew I wouldn't say no to, the exact same three places I always picked to honeymoon to when I used to play MASH in middle school. Jamaica is where we honeymooned and we always talked about going back. We wanted to go for our thirtieth birthdays but decided to pull the goalie so to say and try to get pregnant so the trip got postponed. Four years later and it still hasn't happened. Australia, the one continent I've always wanted to go to, but have never even seriously considered it. The top of my bucket list is to see a baby koala in its homeland. And Maine, I laugh in my head, because it's a silly bucket list location but when I was young, I remember the local weatherman advertising a fall foliage trip to Maine. When my parents asked my sister and my input for our summer vacation, I obviously stated Maine. Needless to say, it wasn't our summer destination and although I don't know much about the state, I still long to go there.

Scrunching my eyebrows, I shake my head. "Um, none of those are equal to Cooperstown." I pause then hold my finger up, wagging it back and forth. "Don't even think you're going to buy some kind of historical baseball memorabilia and that will even out a trip to Jamaica."

Shawn's smile softens as he sits up, slightly shaking his head. "No, babe, not at all. I just want you to be treated like the princess you are and I know you'd love to visit any of those places."

My eyes tear up and I bury my head against his shoulder. So many emotions have ran through my body in the past day and it's all finally catching up to me. I hold onto my husband for dear life because he is my anchor.

"I didn't mean to make you cry, Jules. I just want to give you the world because you deserve it and now, I finally can," Shawn whispers in my ear as he rubs my back.

BABY, MAYBE

This man would make a wonderful father. I can picture him with our little girl, dancing in the kitchen with her while she stands on his feet and he treats her like the princess she is. I have never wanted something so bad in my life that I have had zero control over and couldn't make happen. Fifty thousand dollars or not, still doesn't change the fact that neither of us can complete our family the way it should be.

CHAPTER 7

Mixed into the background music playing Alvin and the Chipmunks Christmas CD, Shawn's newest nephew, only six months old, cries in his mother's arms as his older cousins run past him, screaming and shooting Nerf guns. Their fathers, along with my husband, are in the living room playing their annual Texas Hold 'Em tournament while their mothers, and myself, prepare the annual Christmas dinner.

"Vannah, if you'd stop nursing him, he'd start sleeping through the night," Savannah's mother, a woman in her sixties, states, taking the little boy from her and bouncing him up and down.

"Mother, there's no evidence that breast milk or formula helps a child to sleep through the night," Savannah retorts, hovering over her child as though the woman holding him didn't raise her herself.

"I'm just saying, I took you all off the boob at six weeks on the dot and you all started sleeping through the night right away," the elderly woman explains very matter-of-factly.

Savannah, Shawn's cousin, looks over at me and rolls her eyes. I smile sympathetically although I have nothing to sympathize with because I've never had a baby to know what helps him sleep through the night or not.

Across the room, Shawn's mother, Juanita Hampton, clears her throat, causing all of us to look in her direction. Once she's satisfied that she has everyone's attention, the same grin that my husband has adorns her face. Shawn is much cuter when he wears it, when Juanita does it, she just looks smug.

"Well, Steven and Alexis aren't here to share but... I'm going to be a grandmother again!"

Her announcement makes my stomach drop. The other women in the room squawk and throw up their arms in excitement. I flick the peeler faster and faster against the potato in my hand, trying not to let any of the tears fall from my eyes. Alexis is Shawn's older sister who already has three kids with two different men. Every time she gets pregnant, Juanita reacts the same way with the big announcement and it's only a matter of time before she asks me to throw yet another baby shower for her.

Tears cloud my vision and I scrap faster at the potato until a hand covers mine. When I glance up, Savannah is holding her baby boy on one hip and touching my hand with her free one. I blink quickly, trying to hide my frustration, and force a smile to my face.

"Easy on that potato, Jules, I don't think it did anything to you," Savannah says with a smile.

She reminds me a lot of Shawn. She's probably almost a decade younger than us but still one of the most mature women in the family. While we never told anyone about our fertility issues, Juanita took it upon herself to inform the family of our business. I just thank my lucky stars that none of them have ever asked me about it.

I shrug, dropping the potato and peeler into the bowl on the counter. "Sorry, I just got so excited about Alexis' fourth kid on the way," I say dryly, immediately knowing I shouldn't have said anything.

Luckily, Savannah laughs and does a small eye roll.

"Yeah, I feel like we'll see her on one of those talk shows sooner than later running a DNA test on those kids."

I tilt my head and smile at Savannah's effort to make me feel better. The baby reaches up, grabbing at her face and squealing in excitement that he got her nose. I remember a time that I used to find that sort of thing cute but nowadays, I find it more annoying than anything. Sometime while trying to become a mother and have a baby of my own, I became a resentful, bitter woman.

"Thanks," I mutter and Savannah nods, her hand on my shoulder.

"So, I heard that you and Shawn won some money off a lottery ticket?" she asks casually as she changes the subject.

"Not from Juanita," I mumble.

Savannah takes me by surprise as a loud, boisterous laugh slips out of her lips. She tries to cover her mouth but the laughing doesn't stop. Soon, I find myself joining her and even her baby boy is giggling along with us. The rest of the kitchen goes silent, interrupting the fourth baby celebration, but Savannah and I can't seem to stop our giggles. The other women stare at us, appalled that we disturbed their celebration, but the two of us and this adorable little boy don't care. For once, I'm celebrating a pregnancy announcement, if only in a slightly facetious way.

CHAPTER 8

Banished from the kitchen and relieved of my potato duties, Savannah and I enjoy a glass of wine on the sun porch. We can still hear the warbling of the women in the kitchen and the shrieks from the children but it's nice to be away from it all for the time being. Plus, I could really get used to drinking wine again... and all the spontaneous sex we've been having lately. Shawn was right to just let go and live life.

"So, seriously, how much did you win if you don't mind me asking?"

Suddenly embarrassed, I respond quietly, "Fifty thousand."

In slow motion, Savannah turns her head to face me as her jaw drops open. "As in fifty thousand dollars?"

I nod and Savannah shakes her head. "Wow! That's awesome! What are you guys going to do with it?"

"Probably a couple trips, Shawn really wants to go to Cooperstown for the Baseball Hall of Fame. I haven't decided where I want to go on our trip. Then we'll put some in savings and then we're going to finally start the kitchen remodel that we've always been talking about."

Savannah bites her bottom lip and looks away, her

mouth making a small oval and "oh" is all that comes out. I scoot to the edge of my seat, setting my glass of wine on the table between us and lean toward her.

"Oh what?"

She shakes her head, sipping her wine and muttering, "Nothing."

I narrow my eyes, feeling myself get slightly defensive. "No, Savannah, that's not an 'oh nothing.' What did you mean?"

Without turning her body, she glances in my direction. "Well... I just thought that you guys would... spend the money some other way."

Confused, I shake my head. "Like how?"

"Well, are you guys still trying to get pregnant? I thought you'd spend the money on..."

"Fertility treatments?" I finish for her. I've been doing these treatments for years and I still don't know if they're called fertility or infertility treatments. I mean, we're infertile, trying to be fertile, but it honestly doesn't matter because nothing is working to make us more fertile vs infertile.

She shrugs and nods, her cheeks turning red. "Yeah, I'm sorry. Was I supposed to know?"

"Juanita is your aunt," I say, making a statement instead of a question.

The two of us are quiet for a few seconds then we look at each other and start laughing. Between the wine and the family dynamic inside, of which they're *still* discussing Alexis' pregnancy, we're both crying by the time we catch our breath and stop our laughter. I can honestly say I've never laughed this hard at any of Shawn's family gatherings.

"So, are you guys still trying or are you done?" Savannah asks, bringing it back around to the original topic at hand.

I sigh, running my finger around the rim of my glass as I wipe the water from my eyes. "We're still trying but we're taking a break right now." I hold up my wine glass. "I have to say, it's been a pretty great break."

Savannah nods. "I'm sure it'll happen when—"

I hold up my hand to stop her. "Don't, don't say it'll happen when it's supposed to or any form of that statement."

Her cheeks flush and she mutters "sorry."

"No, I'm sorry, I didn't mean to make you feel bad. It's just so emotionally and physically draining. It pushes us apart when treatments don't work, it makes sex automatic and more like a chore, and everything just wears on you, not to mention it's so expensive."

"That's why I thought you all would use the money to do more IVFs or adoption."

Sighing, I shake my head as though it was just that easy and tear up a bit. "Honestly, we didn't even discuss it. We're on a break from trying and Shawn was so excited about the trips and remodel…"

Savannah leans over, pouring more wine in my glass. "Then if you're on a break and we've still got five more hours of family nonsense, let's drink more wine."

Laughing, one lone tear runs down my cheek and I nod. "To Juanita," I toast, holding up my glass.

"And don't forget Alexis," Savannah adds, clinking my glass and our giggle fest continues.

CHAPTER 9

Surrounded by power tools and floor samples, my mind tries to escape as far away as possible. I loathe any type of home improvement store. I don't understand differences of the thickness of plywood and I really couldn't care less. My husband on the other hand is in love with these kinds of places. He could, and has, spent hours walking from one end of the store to the other while I would much rather spend the afternoon in the dentist's chair.

So, instead of looking at samples, my mind drifts to the note that allowed us to shop for the kitchen remodel that our home so desperately needs. Shawn never thought twice about the people that left the lottery ticket on our door, or at least hasn't said anything to me. I think about them all the time and wonder what their note meant. What is their rough patch? What are their day to day issues? Did someone die? Did they lose money? What is it? Shawn would probably say it's just me being nosey but I think it's the compassionate part of my soul that wonders why they're hurting. One thing it proves to me is that you never know who is hurting, looks can be deceiving. So be kind to everyone because we all have something in our life that isn't perfect and is causing us pain.

"Are you thinking wood or tile for the floor?"

"Um, wood."

"Then we'll have to put pads on the bottom of the furniture so we don't scratch up the floor and we'll have to get special cleaner for the floor, too."

"Okay then tile."

"Tile holds a lot of dirt in the grout, we'll have to get on our hands and knees to scrub it."

Sighing, I kiss my husband's cheek. "Shawn, I really don't care."

Not waiting for his response, I wander away from the counter and find myself in the plumbing aisle, wondering what the hell half this stuff is meant for. It makes me count my blessings that I have a man like Shawn to take care of that stuff for me because otherwise, I'd be lost. I try to clear my mind by turning the water on and off on the demo sink, trying to figure out where the water is running to. It isn't until a worker in a navy vest clears his throat that I pull my hand back, feeling like a child caught stealing candy.

One aisle over and I'm in the appliances section, finally understanding what these things do. Not able to fidget with anything, my mind drifts off to another place that it's been in for the last four days. My period is late. I have a plethora of pregnancy tests under the sink at home but I refuse to take one or get my hopes up. I stopped tracking everything, ovulation days, thickness of cervical mucus, my temperature so I'm not even sure that we had sex during the days I was most fertile. I've been racking my brain to try to remember and if my rough calculations are correct then that night after I almost caught the kitchen on fire, we had sex, lots of sex and it was good, during my highest fertile days. However, my period's been late before and I've always been let down by my monthly visitor arriving not too long after, inevitably about an hour after I pee on a stick. For that fact alone, I'm putting off the test as long as possible.

"Jules!" Shawn jogs down the aisle toward me. "Hey, what's wrong, babe?"

I take a deep breath and put my hands on his shoulders. I haven't confided in him that my period's late. No need to get both our hopes up and maybe, I'm a little worried that he'll think I'm interrupting our break. Besides, I've always envisioned some sort of amazing pregnancy reveal to him, letting him know that he'll finally be a father. Unfortunately with fertility, or infertility, treatments, everything is so precise and timed that there is no element of surprise.

Smiling, I shake my head. "Nothing's wrong. You know I just hate this stuff so why don't you make all the decisions and know that I'll love it?"

Shawn frowns. "Did you decide where you wanted to take your trip yet?"

Kissing him softly, I shake my head. "Not yet but you'll be the first to know when I do."

He nods. "This is our money, Julie, so I just want you to enjoy it, too."

"Build me that kitchen and I'll enjoy it lots when it's all done."

Shawn gives a half smile and I push his softly. "Go build our dream home. I'll be in the…" I point toward the front of the store. "…organization aisle, looking for totes."

He grabs my waist, pulling my body to his and plants his lips on mine. I run my hand over his head, oddly aroused at making out in the middle of the home improvement store. Grinning as he pulls away, I wiggle my fingers in a wave as he heads back to the flooring aisle. A random cramp jumps through my stomach and the panic sets in that Aunt Flo might be here. Looking around quickly, I search for the restroom sign, praying that my period isn't here. If we don't have to pay for any more fertility treatments, imagine the nursery we could plan. Now, that is a home improvement project I could get on board with!

CHAPTER 10

Three more hours and the end of yet another year that I'm not pregnant will end. A holiday that I used to love as a teenager, because it was the one night a year that my parents actually let me stay out past midnight, has now become just another night. The page of the calendar flips over and the only difference is that it states a new year. The battles don't disappear at midnight, the heartaches from the year before aren't healed, and it's only a matter of time before the positivity of a new year is defeated. I hate to be a pessimist but I'm at a point in my life where I prefer to be real over faking that rainbows and unicorns exist.

The one positive thing about infertility is that Shawn and I have made some amazing friends in the process. After being a silent sufferer, I turned to blogging to let out my emotions of how unfair it was that we weren't getting pregnant while it seemed as though the rest of the world was getting knocked up without even having sex. Through the blogging community, I found so many other couples experiencing the same things we were although each of our stories are silently different. While the women socialize to commiserate together, the men typically give a few head nods to acknowledge the one thing they have in common then move on to other interests they share such as sporting teams, hunting, and bacon. So, while I'd much rather be sitting at home in my pajamas watching the ball drop, our little community has banded together for a game night at one of our friends' house to ring in the new year, childfree, and with plenty of alcohol to begin the new year with a horrible hangover.

"Here, babe, I got you an Angry Orchard, I know you love cider beer," Shawn says, kissing my cheek and letting me smell his own beer on his breath.

Shaking my head, I wave the drink off. "It's not cider beer, it's just hard cider."

My husband rolls his eyes. "Just like deer burger isn't 'burger,' it's just venison. Whatever, you know what I mean, now drink up!"

I smile in adoration at the ridiculous things we argue over. It's things like hard cider vs cider beer that define a couple and their inside jokes. Leaning forward, I press my lips against Shawn's, enjoying the moment of the little things in life. He moans in my mouth, unable to touch me with his hands since he's holding a drink in each hand. Pulling away, he holds the bottle out to me again.

"How about we get drunk and have wild, crazy, unprotected sex tonight?"

I shake my head laughing as he wiggles his eyebrows, thinking he's hilarious. It isn't the first time he's made this comment but in the past, he likes to say it when we're in a very public place and no one knows us. He's the strong one between us, the one that makes me laugh through this whole chapter of our lives.

"I'm game for the last part but I'm not drinking tonight," I try to say as casually as possible.

Shawn sighs, his silliness fading. "Why not? We're on a break, Jules, remember? We agreed to let loose and enjoy the holidays?" He cocks his eyebrow. "It's still the holidays, okay?"

I nod, biting my bottom lip, still not sure if I should mention anything about my period that still hasn't arrived. "I know but I just want to start off the new year feeling good and not all gross from drinking too much. You know what they say, the way you start the new year is how the rest of it will go."

Shawn shakes his head. "You're lying. You don't believe in New Year's and the start of something fresh. Now, tell me the truth, wife... 'till death do us part, remember?"

Glancing around the room, I grab Shawn's hand and walk us outside. No way do I want this to be overheard by any person in that room, I know it would cause so much heartache. Barely outside, with the door shut behind us, my teeth are already chattering. Shawn wraps his big arms around me, trying to warm me up.

"What is it, Jules?"

"I... I'm... late," I say through chattering teeth and nerves.

Shawn narrows his eyebrows and I know what he's thinking. He's heard this before, it's nothing new. I've been late and it's nothing. This is exactly why I didn't say anything sooner.

"Oookaaay..." he says, drawing it out and allowing him time to think of a better response. "So, how late are you?"

"A week," I whisper and his eyes go wide, because he knows it's the latest I've ever been.

"Wow," he reacts and follows up with, "Have you taken a pregnancy test yet?"

Biting my bottom lip, I shake my head, still shivering in his arms. I snuggle closer against his body, both from the temperature and the fear of the unknown of whatever the hell my body is doing, be it growing a baby or just messing around with me.

"Does it add up? Did we have sex when you were ovulating? Do you really think you might be pregnant?" Shawn asks all these questions in the same breath and it makes me fall a little bit more in love with him to see his excitement.

"Well, we *are* 'taking a break,'" I say, taunting him with my words and a smile under the last moonlight of the year. "But, based on my rough calculations, if I am pregnant, this baby was conceived after I almost burnt down our house."

Shawn lets out a loud whoop, picking me up and swinging me in a circle. His cheering doesn't diminish and it definitely doesn't stop either. I would venture to say that he is probably more excited about this news than when we scratched off the lottery ticket that put fifty thousand dollars in our bank account. Abruptly, Shawn stops the spinning and sets me down, grabbing me by the waist.

"Oh, sorry, babe, I was excited but I don't want to hurt the baby." He leans forward and kisses me. "Come on." He grabs my hand and walks us toward the street where we parked the car.

"Where are we going?" I ask, trying to keep up with him as he's walking quickly from all the emotion. I understand where he's coming from but typically, he's not the one to get this overwhelmed at the possibility.

"To the drug store, you're going to pee on a stick." Shawn stops when we get to the car, handing me the keys then taking my face in both his hands. "I know you don't believe in New Year's and new beginnings but let's either send this year out with some kickass news or leave all the bad news behind us."

Smiling, I nod, because I know it's important to him and he needs something to believe in, we all do. For some of us, it's luck, others it's religion, maybe even silly superstitions like the things we do to ring in the new year. Whatever it is, you gotta have faith in something to give you hope that things will change, that things will be okay, that life will keep on, even when it doesn't seem like it will.

CHAPTER 11

Three minutes until midnight. Three minutes until this year is over. Three minutes until the pregnancy test that I just peed on will tell me if our lives are going to drastically change in the next year. The lone stick sits on the dashboard, neither of us able to sneak a peak unless we move it. The moonlight shines down, casting it in the spotlight and we both stare at the digital numbers on the clock, waiting for next year to come.

Shawn reaches over, taking his hand in mine and squeezing it gently. "You know, if we did make a baby the night you almost burned the house down, that's the night I'd want it to be."

I look over at Shawn like he has three heads. "Why is that? Because it's easy to remember?"

Even in the dark, I can see his smile as he shakes his head. "No, because we were both carefree and in the moment, loving each other with no agenda. We didn't have sex that night to have a baby, we made love to one another and something beautiful came of it."

"How sex is intended to be," I whisper, tearing up as I think about how far away from that we'd been.

Shawn wipes away my tears and kisses the back of my

hand. "It is and that's what we did."

"Maybe did," I correct him, still too afraid to get my hopes up.

"Why do you always do that?"

"Do what?"

"Maybe did. Baby, you gotta let yourself get excited, be in the moment, even if the moment is only for a short time."

Damn hormones, my eyes glass over again and I shake my head. "I'm too scared to, Shawn. I've lived in the two week wait so many times, letting myself pretend that I am with child, playing out how we'll tell our families, the announcement changing with each holiday and season that I might potentially be pregnant. I've felt that grief month after month and I'm so scared of hurting as much as I have in the past."

Shawn squeezes my hand. "But it's the past, Jules, and this could be the last time we experience that. Now, close your eyes and pretend with me."

I glance over at my husband, my eyes still thick with wetness. He leans his head back against his seat and shuts his eyes. Taking a deep breath, I do the same thing and squeeze his hand when my eyes are closed.

"Now, when this test says you're pregnant. Who will be the first person you tell?"

My eyes may only see darkness but vivid images race through my mind. Each one I've seen before when I've pictured telling our families and friends but none of them an actual reality. My mind still running, I hit the mental pause button, trying to focus on just one.

"Candace."

Even with my eyes closed, I can hear the smile in his voice when he responds. "Good choice, she's been a great friend to you over the years."

Nodding, although no one can see me, I get emotional again thinking of all the crazy phone calls I've shared with my sorority sister from so many years ago. Never mind what crazy hour of the day that I call her, she always answers and listens to my rants about pregnant women and my lack of conceiving my own child. So many days when I was in my darkest hour of negative pregnancy tests, failed IVFs, and my period showing up, Candace, mother of two beautiful boys, cursed everything I did and reminded me of how beautiful I am, with child or without.

"What about you?" I ask, trying not to get too caught up in the possibly fleeting moment.

"Josh," Shawn says with a light squeeze because he knows I'm not a fan of his friend, Josh, but like Candace, he's seen Shawn through some of his darkest days.

I open my eyes, turning my body to face Shawn, my head still resting on my seat. "How will we tell our families?"

Shawn turns his head to me, his eyes open. "You'll be twelve weeks in March? Maybe something geared around St. Patrick's Day?"

"Do you think we should wait longer than twelve weeks? Dr. O said twenty is safer."

"There's no way in hell I'd be able to keep my mouth shut until twenty weeks!" Shawn says with a laugh and I join him. Not since the first few months we tried to get pregnant, years ago, have we ever talked like this. We keep the conversation going for longer than three minutes, discussing everything from names to nurseries. Finally, when the light of the drug store goes off about an hour later, Shawn looks at me with his eyebrows raised.

"Should we look?"

Hesitating, I bite my bottom lip as my stomach churns and I think I might throw up. Shawn reaches on the dashboard, picking up the pregnancy test and holding it between us. He looks up at me and asks if I'm ready. I nod and he counts to three, flipping the test over. In a matter of seconds, my heart is in my throat and tears blur my eyes. Shawn drops the test, moving his hand behind my head and pulling me toward him so he can kiss my forehead.

"I'm so sorry, baby. I thought for sure that it would be positive," he whispers.

I nod, trying to mutter "me, too" but I'm not sure how much of that really gets out. Shawn holds me tenderly, telling me it'll be okay and that we still have each other. My body does whatever it wants, forcing me to sob loudly, soaking Shawn's shirt. In the midst of my breakdown, I'm far too tuned in when my stomach cramps and I know my period is making it's grand entrance any time now, it was just waiting for me to pee on a stick as another slap in the face.

Sitting up, I wipe my tears and take a few deep breaths, regaining my composure. "What if we used the money for a baby?"

Shawn rubs my thigh. "What? What are you talking about?"

"The fifty thousand. What if we used it for a baby?"

"Like buy one off the black market?" Shawn asks, trying to make light of my suggestion.

Rolling my eyes, I shake my head. "No, not off the black market. It's not going to take all of that money to remodel the kitchen. Let's meet with our doctor again, figure out a game plan and weigh our options."

"Jules, we've done that… and done that… and done that. Why do you think this time is different?"

"Because, Shawn, it's a new year and a new beginning. We have way more money than we ever had before to spend on this. This is our year, Shawn, this is the year we have a baby."

Chuckling, Shawn shakes his head. "I thought you didn't believe in the new year, new start bullshit."

With a big grin on my face, I lean forward, kissing my husband for the first time this year. "Well, it's a new attitude for me since it's a new year. What do you say? Can we use some of the money for a baby?"

Running his finger down my cheek, Shawn nods.

"Whatever you want, babe. It's your money as much as mine so let's do it."

I squeal, probably a bit too loudly for the small space we're in. Twisting my body like some sort of contortionist, I move over the console and onto my husband's lap in the passenger seat. Still keeping with the mentally we ended the year on, my husband and I make love in the front seat of our car. First thing tomorrow, more baby research will begin. This is our year, the year we become parents.

CHAPTER 12

"You're up early," Shawn says, setting a cup of coffee on the end table beside my big brown, comfy chair and kissing my cheek.

Staring at my laptop, I jot down some notes in my journal and wave my hand. "No coffee for me but thanks, babe."

Shawn scoffs and puts his fingers under my chin, lifting my head to look at him. "No coffee and up before the sun? Who are you and what did you do to my wife?"

I smile and turn my head slightly, kissing the palm of his hand. "New year, new start, right?" I pat the cushion I'm sitting on as it's wide enough for two people. Shawn slides in sideways next to me, draping his arm over my shoulders and nodding toward my laptop.

"We'll see how long you keep that up. What are you working on?"

Turning to Shawn, I start off slowly, telling him about what I've been doing. "I decided to start over with our research on how to grow our family. It seems ridiculous that we have the mindset that IVF is the only way we'll ever have a kid. We could do embryo adoption, use a surrogate, try a sperm or egg donor or both, adoption, foster, the list goes on, Shawn. Now that we have the funds, we aren't limited."

My voice gets a little faster as I list off each option. Pointing to the screen, I show him the page I'm reading. "This adoption agency's average placement is six-eight months after you're approved. We could get a baby from Missouri, Arkansas, Kansas, Iowa, or Nebraska."

"What about Illinois? What's wrong with a baby Illini? I think that's a little discriminatory," Shawn says playfully.

I roll my eyes. "It's not discriminatory. Those are just the states that this agency works with."

He kisses the side of my head. "I don't know about adoption, Jules. I mean, all these people coming into our home to judge whether or not we're fit to be parents. I'm not really okay with that."

"I know, it makes me nervous, too, but it's for the safety of the child, potentially *our* child. They don't want an innocent child placed with some kind of family like Jeffrey Dahmer."

"I get it, it makes sense, but it's still so… judgmental. Plus, if I'm being completely honest, I'm a little scared that I won't feel a connection to the baby."

I sigh, trying not to let my hope be extinguished. "Okay, well, what about embryo adoption? If couples have extra embryos that they don't want to use, they'll put them up for adoption. The kids won't biologically be ours but I'll carry it like I would our own… or we could use a surrogate if we felt like we had a better chance that way."

I glance over at Shawn, who still doesn't look sold on the idea so I keep talking before he gets a chance to drop any more negativity. Quickly, I click to another website I have open. "Okay, what about sperm or egg donors? Look at this egg donor… she's five-ten, played collegiate volleyball, and is an entrepreneur that runs her own fitness company."

"She sounds nothing at all like you, Jules."

Laughing, I nod. "Yeah, she's got all the good qualities

that I don't have."

Shawn rubs his hand up and down my arm. "But I want *our* baby to have all of your qualities, the good *and* the bad."

"Fine." I maneuver to another website. "What about this sperm donor? His profile says he has dark skin, brown eyes, and dimples like yours."

With a boisterous laugh, Shawn shakes his head. "That sounds like every African American man I know except for the dimples part. How are we supposed to pick a donor based off the basic information provided? How do we know they aren't a serial killer or something?"

I narrow my eyes. "They run background checks on all the donors. Besides, look here, it says he likes sports, especially baseball just like you."

Shawn shakes his head. "Just because he likes sports doesn't mean he's an athlete, there's a big difference there. I want my kid to crank homeruns out of the park at every at bat, not just to like cheering for the guy that does."

I roll my eyes. "When was the last time you cranked one out of the park in your beer league?"

He opens his mouth to object then starts laughing at the truth behind my statement. "Fair enough, babe, fair enough. Look, all I'm saying is that I understand there's plenty of options out there to start a family but I'd really like for us to start a family beginning with us. We've got fifty grand and if we have to do five IVFs to get pregnant, we can."

I give a soft smile and nod. "I get it, Shawn. It's hard to think of our family being anything other than a part of the two of us but it's time to face reality. That might not be a possibility for us, we need to explore other options."

Shawn squeezes his arm around me, pulling me into his lap. "You're right, I'm sorry. Let's just try one more IVF then if that doesn't work, I promise to have a more open mind."

Cupping his cheek, I smile and lean forward to kiss

him. "That sounds like an awesome plan."

Shawn grins, his hand running over my hip and behind my thigh. "But can we still keep trying to the good 'ole fashion way?"

"You mean wild, crazy, unprotected sex?"

Shawn's deep laughs fills the room and my body bounces against his. "Exactly... starting now."

Then in one swift move, Shawn is standing up and carrying me up the stairs to our bedroom. He dips his head, nibbling on my ear and I tilt my head back. Life may not have gone exactly how I planned, hell, not even close, but I wouldn't trade any of it for the world, especially not this man, my knight in shining armor.

CHAPTER 13

The sun shines down from high in the sky, warming my skin on this breezy spring day. One foot in front of another, I pound the pavement, putting miles between the start of my run and the end. I can barely hear the cheers from St. Patty's Day fans who are celebrating the day by drinking green beer instead of running this 5K. Katy Perry blares in my ears, motivating me to keep going and beat my personal record.

The same thought that always creeps into my mind does today as well and I smile. Back in high school, when we were forced to run, I hated it and did everything I could to get out of it. Now, I'll schedule my entire day around making sure I get in a run or sometimes two. Somehow, in my warped mind, I decided that I would give running a try because it was something I could control. I can't tell my body to get pregnant but I can tell myself to go run five miles.

Making the last turn on the course, I see the finish line at the opposite end of the road. I pick up the pace, jogging a little faster. As the flags come into view, I see the pink shirt lady that I've been trading places with the entire race. I started out in front then she snuck up on me and passed me at the first mile. I lagged behind her just enough to keep pace then I lost her at the last hill because hills are not my friend. Now is my moment though, I can catch her and I can leave her in my dust. Cranking my speed up, I dig deep and push myself as hard as I can. Her pink shirt gets closer as does the finish line and just when I don't think I'll step foot across the end before her, my runner's kick burst into full gear and I easily breeze past her just seconds before she does.

As much as I'd love to smile and celebrate my victory, I'm huffing and puffing too hard. I keep walking, trying to catch my breath when I feel his big arms circling my body and lifting me up, celebrating for me. Shawn swings me around, kissing my cheek.

"Wow, Jules, that was amazing! You totally blindsided that lady!"

Half smiling, half still trying to not be winded, I nod and speak in spurts. "I know… I really did… didn't I?"

Shawn laughs, setting me down but keeping his hands on my hips. Leaning his head down to my ear, he whispers, "It got me all hot and bothered to see you like that."

Smiling, I shake my head and try to push him away. "Ew, I'm all hot and sweaty. There is no way that is remotely attractive at all."

"Exactly. You're already all worked up. I could help you with that cool down exercise."

I smirk and cock an eyebrow. "I don't think there would be much cooling down."

Shawn shakes his head, dropping his mouth so he can kiss my neck. I still don't see how he can find me attractive in this moment but I don't mind the sensations he creates with his kisses. It's amazing how when we took the pressure off ourselves, how much our relationship improved. Ever since he implemented that break back at Christmas, our sex lives have been phenomenal.

"As much as I want my husband right now, I really want some ice cold water and a shower."

Shawn groans. "Fine but can I join in the shower?"

Laughing, I untangle myself from him and shake my head. "We'll see."

Skipping the green beer line, I grab a water and we head back home. Shawn replaying the scene from the finish line no less than five more times by the time we pull in the driveway. Still exhausted from my run, I just sit in the car, trying to muster up the energy to walk to the front door. From the passenger side of his SUV, I stare at that red door of ours where the lottery ticket was taped but I don't think about the money we won, I still think about the people that put it there.

I've always read articles and seen documentaries where winning money changes people's lives. Don't get me wrong, fifty-thousand dollars is no small sum of money but our lives haven't changed. Shawn's working on the kitchen remodel, saving some money by doing most of it himself, and neither of us have planned either of the trips we discussed. Sitting in the bank is the rest of the money, waiting for us to make a decision about the future of our family.

Following my gaze to the front door, Shawn knows exactly what I'm thinking about. "Have you made an appointment with a RE yet?"

RE, one of the many acronyms of fertility. RE is reproductive endocrinologist. We've had so many over the years, Shawn can't keep up with which one we're currently seeing. It's not that any of them are under qualified or don't know what they're doing but it's been my mentality that if one can't get us pregnant then jump to the next one, maybe they can do something bigger, better than the last, maybe even be successful! So far, that hasn't worked for me at all.

Still staring at the front door, picturing that card taped to the front door, I shake my head. "Not yet…"

"Really? Why not?" Shawn asks, his voice a mix of surprise and a tiny bit of relief because he knows what kind of crazy I get during treatments.

Tearing my eyes off the front door, I slowly turn to face him. "Because I'm scared."

"Scared? Of what, babe?" Shawn reaches over and takes my hand.

"This is it, Shawn. If this next IVF doesn't work, I'm done. No more treatments, no adoption, no donors. If I don't get pregnant then we aren't meant to have children."

Shawn squeezes my hand as he shakes his head. "Come on, Jules, don't say that. I told you I'd keep my mind open if it didn't work and we could look into more options."

"No, Shawn. I don't want to. I'm tired of living life period to period, censoring who I'm around and when I can and can't drink. I want to try one more time and then I want to be done."

He nods slowly, letting my words sink in. "Okay, that's fair. I'm on board with whatever you decide." He lifts my hand to his mouth and kisses my knuckles. "But why haven't you made an appointment yet?"

I take a deep breath. "Because I'm scared. Life is good right now, Shawn, really good. You and I, we're in a great place. Physically I'm in the best shape of my adult life and mentally, I'm happier than I've been in a long time. Once we make that appointment and start treatments, it's like a ticking time bomb. If it works, we diffuse the bomb and our world gets even better. If it doesn't work, the bomb explodes and everything we've worked so hard for the last few months and the happy place I've been in will be gone. I don't know if I'll be able to recover if this doesn't work, Shawn, that's what I'm scared of."

He takes my face in both his hands and shakes his head. "You'll recover, Julie, we both will. We're in this together, 'til death do us part, remember? Baby or not, we're a family, you and me. We've got this, Jules, no matter if the bomb explodes or not, we've got this. Understand?

Don't go telling me you won't recover."

Tears roll down my cheeks and I nod. "We've got this," I repeat.

Shawn smiles and moves his head up and down. "We've got this."

CHAPTER 14

The sight in front of me makes me sick, literally sick to my stomach. Owls and other woodland creatures decorate the church basement, each table labeled after one of those little critters while pond juice and a trail mix bar don the food table. A very pregnant Alexis greets each guest, rubbing her giant belly, the universal bragging rights of pregnant women, and letting them all know to call her Mama Bear.

I guzzle down another cup of pond juice, some kind of mint sherbert punch that actually tastes awful, maybe if it had vodka then it would be better. I unwrap another 'Welcome Baby' mini candy bar, grateful that I finally found a Mr. Goodbar. I throw it in my mouth and try to focus on my irritation instead of the sadness I'm experiencing. It's been a good run, I found my happy place at the start of the year and after five months, I was really starting to believe in that whole new year, new start crap. Then I got the invitation for the Mama Bear-to-be and the resentment that I'd pushed away toward all pregnant women came bubbling back. Maybe if it was Alexis' first baby, I wouldn't feel this way but it's her *fourth* in five years, what more could the woman need???

"Whoa, take it easy there, tadpole, or you might turn into a frog prematurely."

Forcing myself to look away from Mama Bear Alexis, I smile when I see Savannah standing beside me. She reaches out and gently takes the pond juice away from me as though I'm some kind of recovering pond juice-aholic. The cup safely out of my grasp, I throw my arms around her and hug her tightly, relieved someone from my side is here.

"Thank god you showed up!"

"Why wouldn't I?" Savannah asks, narrowing her eyes in confusion.

"Juanita said you didn't RSVP."

Savannah throws up her hand, waving it back and forth. "Oh yeah, she texted me… a few hundred times about that. After the third text, I vowed I wasn't going to respond just to prove a point."

We both start to laugh, getting a bit loud and when I look across the room, Juanita is giving us a dirty look. I cover my mouth, trying to stifle my laughter. When I look back at Savannah, I try to slyly nod in my mother-in-law's direction. "I'd say mission accomplished."

Savannah grins proudly. "Good. Now, tell me what you've been up to since Christmas."

"Well—"

"Julie, do you have the game?"

Like a ninja, Juanita appears out of nowhere and interrupts us. Her hands on her hips and the way she's tapping her foot makes me want to lie and tell her I forgot it at home. However, knowing she gave birth to the man I love, I nod and force a smile to my face. I hand her a folder and a bag of pens.

"Here you go, one woodland animals word search."

My monster-in-law, something I've never called her until this moment, scoffs and shakes the folder. "That's it? That's all you came up with?"

My face flushes and immediately, my blood pressure

spikes. Speaking in my loudest whisper so as not to draw attention to us, I lean forward to make sure Juanita hears me loud and clear. "I'm sorry, *Mother*. When I had guests guess the size of Alexis' belly at the first shower, she was offended and told everyone I was calling her fat. At the second shower, when I put candy bars in diapers, Alexis' made me throw them away because it made her queasy. Then at the *third* shower, when I did the Mom or Dad Quiz, you told me I was making Alexis feel like an awful mother because everyone picked the dad to do the most with the baby then her. So, I figured for the FOURTH shower, doing a word search puzzle shouldn't offend Alexis in any way. So, please, Juanita, forgive me for being so insensitive as to the caliber of baby shower game you expected."

When I finish speaking my piece, something I've said in my mind so many times, but never thought I'd ever say out loud, my heart is beating wildly and I can barely hear my own voice because the thump of my heart is so loud in my ears. My chest puffs up and down and Juanita stares at me, her face stricken with disbelief at my audacity. Without a word, she spins on her heel and marches to the center of the room, holding the folder high in the air.

"Game time, everyone!" she calls to the group and begins to distribute the word search.

"Ho-ly shit," Savannah mutters and it's a relief to know I haven't lost my hearing.

I glance over at her, suddenly horrified at what I just said to the woman that I have to share every holiday with for the rest of my life. "Oh... my... god... what did I just do?"

"You were just totally badass!" Savannah grabs my hand, pulling me into the kitchen and out of the sight of everyone else. "You just put Juanita in her place and shut her down. Oh my god, Julie, that was so fuckin' awesome! Can I say fuckin' in the church basement? I don't care because that's what it was and there's no other substitute for that word. So badass! Man, I wish I were you, you're my new hero!"

Savannah is dancing around me in a circle, like I'm some kind of rock star. Meanwhile, I start to feel lightheaded and look for a place to sit down. My head spinning, I just slide down the wall and take a seat on the floor. A few seconds later, Savannah is beside me.

"Shawn will kill me," I whisper, cradling my head in my arms as I lean them against my knees.

"No, he won't. His mother has driven him nuts forever. Like your mother does you, like I'll do to my kids and like you'll do to yours. It's what moms do best, they can't let go of their babies so they drive us all insane."

Tears fill my eyes and I look over at her. "You really think I'll be a mom some day?" Not that it really matters what she thinks, like it'll change the course of our story, but sometimes it's that extra boost that someone besides your husband thinks you'll be a parent.

"Hell yeah and you'll be a great one, too. That kid will adore you and you'll spoil it rotten. Then, he or she will grow up and you'll make him or her batty. It's called the circle of life, baby."

Savannah lays her head on my shoulder and I lie mine on top of hers, contemplating her words and the ugly words I spewed at Juanita. How can a woman that loves the same man as much as I do be so hateful and insensitive to me? I want nothing more than to make her son happy, give him a child, and all she wants to do is make sure her own daughter has the perfect baby shower game. My mind wanders back to Savannah's comments and I nod my head.

"My mom drives me nuts, too. Last year, she told me she'd take me out to dinner for my birthday. When I texted her to set up the plans, she told me that she'd made chili so you know what she gave me for my birthday? Gas."

Savannah looks up at me. "Sounds like a shitty

birthday."

My eyes meet hers and immediately, we break out into our laughter that we've grown so accustom to. All my emotions mix together and tears run down my cheeks as we both laugh like hyenas. A couple minutes of this and my stomach is cramping from the laughter workout. With her perfect timing, Juanita steps into the kitchen and glares down at us.

"I hate to break up your little party in here but Alexis is about to open her gifts."

Wiping at my eyes, I stand up, smoothing out my dress and marching behind my mother-in-law, Savannah on my heels. As we join the rest of the guests, Alexis is holding up the plain pink bag with my gift in it. I'm reusing the bag from when the girls at work gave me my birthday present last year, I wasn't going to go drop five bucks on a specific baby shower bag that will only wind up in the trash.

"This is from my favorite sister-in-law, Julie," Alexis says, plastering on the fakest smile I've ever seen as she plucks away at the tissue paper. "I wonder what she could've gotten me..." She pauses to peek inside the bag, her smile dissolving as she snaps her head up and scowls in my direction. "Diapers? You got me diapers?"

"Um... yes. Babies need diapers, right? Or did that change?" I ask, trying to joke about it and being thoroughly confused as to why she's upset that I got her diapers.

"Yes, babies need diapers," she huffs, tossing the bag in the heap of other gifts she's already opened.

She picks up the next gift and I should probably let it go but I can't stop myself from asking, "So, what's wrong with diapers?"

Alexis looks up, lasers almost shooting out her eyes and melting me right in front of her. "You won the lottery and all you got your sister-in-law was diapers?"

My stomach sinks and I'm in too much shock to even retaliate with an answer. It has been no secret that Shawn and I won from that scratch-off ticket but not once, not ever, has anyone in his family, other than Savannah, so much as said congratulations. Now, suddenly, I'm the bad guy because I only bought her diapers for a shower gift which is the exact same thing I got the three kids of hers before this.

Savannah's hand moves to my back, trying to console me as I finally notice fat, crocodile tears running down my cheeks. Alexis is on to the next gift, already over mine and all that it lacked. Trying not to draw any more attention to myself, I tiptoe toward the exit, grab my purse, and walk to the parking lot, knowing that this is the last baby shower of Alexis' I ever attend, even if she has fifty-thousand more kids.

Pacing back and forth and taking deep breaths, I pull out my phone and type two words. I've been putting off our appointment with our RE, too afraid to leave my happy place, but now that I've seen the other side of it, I'm ready to move forward. My mind hasn't changed, this is it. If I don't get pregnant this time around, we're done trying. Hovering my finger over the send button, I close my eyes, channeling my inner-maternal instinct that I know is hidden deep inside me. A feeling of peacefulness washes over me and I open my eyes, staring at the beautiful lilies in front of me and I know now's the time. Hitting send, I text my husband two words, two little words that will change our future... *I'm ready*.

Ready or not, now's the time...

CHAPTER 15

"Well, Julie, I have to say that I'm quite impressed at your health right now."

Forcing a smile, I nod politely although internally I'm rolling my eyes so far north that they should probably be stuck there. When it all came down to it, I knew Dr. Valleroy was the best option. She and I may not see eye to eye with her bedside manner but she's the best in the field, there's no doubt about that. She speaks numbers, not emotions, and she's a straight shooter. She doesn't give her patients false hope, she spats out statistics and truth. And if an inkling of your emotions show through, she hands you a box of Kleenex and that's the extent of her emotional support.

Shawn loves her because he's the analytical one in our relationship. Meanwhile, I cried for hours after our first appointment because Dr. Valleroy said we had a fifty-fifty chance of conceiving which in my mind meant it would never work. Now, here we are on our third and final IVF and the fifty-fifty odds haven't worked in our favor… yet. I'm putting my faith in Dr. V and leaving all my cards on the table.

"Thank you. At Christmas, we decided to take a break

from trying to conceive and it really allowed me to focus on myself. I know physically I'm in a much better place and even mentally and emotionally I know I'm better than ever."

It's true. The break was exactly what I needed, what we needed. Six months ago, my marriage was about to fall apart because of these damn fertility, or infertility, whatever you want to call them, treatments. I was about to lose the man who has supported me through my darkest hours. Luckily, he was smart enough for both of us and we couldn't be in a better place now than we've ever been. I focused on running, completing a half-marathon and a handful of 5ks, and now I'm ready for the biggest race in my life.

Dr. Valleroy politely smiles and nods, trying her best to act like she cares when in reality, she's ready to spew a whole bunch of scary and intimidating facts that's going to make me feel anything but confident about this IVF cycle.

"Well, I'm liking all the numbers you've both been reporting. So, once your next period starts, you'll call the office and begin your birth control right away."

She continues on, explaining the next steps of the IVF process. She must have forgot that I'm an old pro at this and with a little bit of schooling, I could probably take her job. The irony isn't lost on me that every cycle starts with birth control, the one thing I've been avoiding for years as we've tried to start our family. Of course now, I'll be anxiously awaiting my period which is another polar opposite of what my life typically has revolved around. It's just another example of how life comes full circle whether you want it to or not.

A couple prescriptions, some stats that I refuse to listen to, and Shawn and I are walking back to our car. I walk around to the passenger side, waiting for him to unlock the door. I'm too deep in thought to pay attention to whether or not he's clicked the key fob so I'm anxiously pulling at the door handle but it isn't opening. When I look up,

Shawn is standing on the sidewalk laughing at me.

"Come on," he says, motioning for me to walk his way.

I frown, unsure what he's up to. Shawn knows I hate surprises or well, the unknown... oh, the irony of that statement. Hesitantly, I walk toward him and when I'm beside him on the sidewalk, he takes my hand and gives it a kiss.

"Let's take a walk," he says, nodding in front of us.

Keeping my guard up, I nod. "Ooo... kay... What are you up to?"

Shawn smiles and shakes his head. "Nothing, I just want to enjoy this beautiful weather with my beautiful bride."

With my free hand, I lift my hair off my neck to get a breeze flowing. Snorting, I shake my head. "Beautiful weather? Since when does ninety degrees with a hundred percent humidity equal beautiful weather?"

Shawn chuckles and squeezes my hand. "Fair enough. I just wanted to see where your mind is. This could be our last consult with Dr. Valleroy. How are you feeling about that?"

I take a deep breath and nod. "Surprisingly, I feel at peace with it. I don't know what it is, a sixth sense, mother's intuition, or what, but I just have this feeling that this needs to be it."

"Like you're going to get pregnant kind of feeling?" Shawn asks, not even bothering to hide the hopefulness in his voice.

Laughing, I shake my head. "Come on, Shawn, you know better than to say that to me." I stop walking and turn to face him, shrugging as I do. "Honestly, I don't feel one way or the other whether this will work or not. Speaking in your language, I feel like we're both physically in better shape than any other cycle we've done before so that's got to work in our favor somehow."

Shawn nods, rubbing his hands up and down my biceps like he would on a cold, winter day. Today is anything but that but he knows I need his touch, his comfort to support me in this decision.

"Jules, you know we've got the money so if it doesn't work this time, we can always try another cycle or look into other options that you'd been researching."

Pushing up on my tippy toes, I rest my hands on my husband's chest and lightly kiss his lips. "I know, babe, but no... this is it. All of the craziness and trying to conceive and all that jazz almost drove us apart. I don't want that, Shawn. Mansion, apartment, shack, or house, I want to experience life with you, kids or not. You're my world, Shawn, and raising a child with you would just be an added bonus of getting to spend my life with you."

He smiles and pushes my hair out of my eyes. "Mansion, apartment, shack, or house... that's my kind of love language." He chuckles at first which grows into a full on belly laugh. In only a matter of seconds, I've joined his laughter. Soon, tears are running down my cheeks but it's not from the laughing.

"I'm going to ask one more time, babe, and then I won't bother you again." Shawn moves his fingers under my chin and lifts my head so I am looking directly into his eyes. "Are you sure this is the last time?"

Tears stream down my face as I'm overcome with so many emotions. Fear that this might not work and I'll never be a mother, fear that it will work and I won't know what the hell I'm doing. Excitement and anticipation of the growing hope that every cycle brings. Hopelessness that everything is out of my control once again and there's nothing I can do other than roll with the punches.

My voice is steady, despite the tears. "Don't make me second guess it, Shawn. I know, deep down, that this is meant to be our last treatment. I have their eery feeling of peacefulness and I know that we'll be okay, no matter how the two week wait goes. Shawn, together, you and I can conquer this world whether we're parents or not."

His face lights up with that big smile I always love to

see. During my darkest days, Shawn would flash this grin, the same exact one I'm staring at right now, and I would know that everything will be fine. That serenity I was feeling grows, relaxing me even more, and I know I'm right. This is it, this is our last cycle. Will we get pregnant? I have no idea. Baby… maybe?

CHAPTER 16

"Babe, what are you doing?"

I glance up from the small spot I'm standing in and nod toward the open pantry. "I'm cleaning out the pantry. What does it look like?"

He chuckles and points to the trash can. "You already cleaned out the pantry, the trash can is overflowing. I don't think any expired items got past you."

"Well, yeah, I threw away the old but now I'm organizing what's left, first by container then by labels. See?"

I wave my hand like Vanna White toward the cans of tomatoes, chili beans, and cream of mushroom soup. Apparently Shawn and I buy ingredients for chili every time we go to the grocery store in addition to a can of cream of mushroom soup because our pantry is overflowing with these items.

Shawn cocks his eyebrow and nods. "Is this what they call nesting?"

I wave my hands and shake my head. "Don't say that, don't jinx us!"

Shawn walks to me, pushing my arms to my side and

squeezing my shoulders. "Jules, you know me saying that has no effect on whether or not this cycle will work."

Lifting my shoulders up and down, I shrug him off and turn back to alphabetizing our canned goods. "Whatever, just let me do me, whatever it takes to keep my mind off the elephant in the room."

Nodding, Shawn starts to back away from the space I'm currently organizing. "Fair enough."

He's almost out of the room when I call to him. "Babe? I want us to start a Japanese cleanse."

Slowly, he turns to face me, his lips dipped into a frown. "Does that mean we have to drink lemon juice and apple cider vinegar or some concoction like that?"

"No, it's this thing I read about. Every day, we each get rid of one item that doesn't bring us happiness."

My husband crinkles his nose in the way that always drives me crazy. "Isn't that like feng shui?"

I throw up my hands, exasperated that he's making such a big deal out of it. "I don't know what it is but it makes me feel better!"

In a few swift steps, Shawn's hands are back on my arms, applying pressure against my biceps and I feel myself start to calm down. Like running into a brick wall, I'm slammed in the face with the reality of what I've been saying. Tears fall down my cheeks and Shawn wraps his arms around my body, pulling me close to him and smoothing out my hair.

"Jules, this is the just the start of the cycle and all the drugs. I know what you're doing, you've done it after every cycle that hasn't worked. It's not going to be like that this time, babe, this time is different."

"How do you know that, Shawn?" I growl at him, my hormones flaring up out of nowhere. "You don't! Just because we won the lottery, doesn't mean we'll be on the positive side of Dr. Valleroy's fifty percent this time."

Shawn lifts my chin up, looking me directly into my eyes. It's like the man has a way of staring deep into my soul that calms me and puts me back in check. He smiles and moves his head up and down.

"Look, all I need you to do is rest and make the perfect little home for our sweet baby, okay? I'll Japanese cleanse and label the pantry if you will just sit down and take it easy. Deal?"

"Shawn... it's day ten of lupron shots and I haven't had my bleed yet."

The things I know and how in touch I am with my body makes me want to roll my eyes. I wish I didn't have to count shots or days or know exactly when my body is supposed to bleed but I do. Every time I give myself a shot, I think about the drunk couples that forget to use protection and wind up with a child nine months later or the couple who got pregnant because the condom broke. Meanwhile, I've had unprotected sex pretty much every other day for the last few years and am now injecting myself with more meds than a nurse working a double shift and I'm still not with child. It's frustrating when I do everything exactly as I've been told and it doesn't work. Today is day ten of lupron, the first of many medicines I'll be on. Day ten is when your body is supposed to bleed, like your period. If it doesn't come, the entire cycle is cancelled and devastated doesn't even begin to explain how I'll feel.

I've had tears pretty much off and on the past couple days all over this bleed. Today though, they've been non-stop, even as I was creating my own Dewey Decimal system for our pantry. My eyelashes are clumped together, my eyeballs are bloodshot and my throat hurts from all the crying. The sad thing is that this is just part of the process.

Shawn nods, knowing there is nothing he can say to make me feel better. His lips press against my forehead and he whispers, "I'll go run you a bath."

Ten minutes later, I'm trying my best to relax in a tub of warm water and bubble bath. Staring at my toes, I dip them back and forth into the water, watching it make small waves. Tears silently roll down my cheeks and I don't try to stop them. I'm so pissed off at my body right now. In all my adult life, since I got my period in fifth grade, I have *never* missed a period, not once, not ever have I ever even thought I might be pregnant. Sure, in my head I would draw it out that I might be late in an effort to think I was pregnant but in reality, I knew I never was. I've never had a pregnancy scare in my life, which I used to be thankful for, but on a day like today, it irritates me that I'll never know what it's like.

I'm stressed, like super stressed, and Shawn is right, I should be anything but that. I should be relaxing and lying on the couch, letting my body do the work except that it's not working. Call it non-mother's intuition but I am simply not feeling it this cycle. If this lupron bleed doesn't come then we're in a holding pattern and I honestly don't know what we'll do next. It's scary enough to go through fertility treatments but knowing it's your last one, that this is a "Hail Mary," that it's this or nothing, is enough to scar you for life. When we sat through our orientation class a few years ago and they spouted off the statistic that one-two couples in our class would have a cancelled cycle, I never thought it would be us. Then again, I never thought we'd have to do fertility treatments either. Isn't life just grand?

My toes still splashing around in the water, I notice that my tears have stopped although my sadness still lingers. I tilt my head back against the tub and sink further into the water, sloshing my head back and forth so I can hear the water moving. It always amazes me at how far away everything seems when you're underwater. Lots of things amaze me, for instance, us winning the lottery. To this day, just shy of a year later, with the majority of our winnings either in savings, paid toward fertility treatments, or dedicated to our kitchen remodel, I still wonder why we won the money. When I read about the odds of winning money in the amount we did, it's way less than fifty-fifty. So then I find myself resentful toward us winning the lottery and not the baby pool. It's a vicious cycle that I live in and in a way, I guess I should consider myself lucky that this is the last time I'll be experiencing it.

Using my toe, I push the drain stopper in the tub to let the water run out. On autopilot, I get out of the tub and dry off, making my way to our bedroom. Suddenly, out of nowhere, I get that 'period feeling' and drop my towel, racing to the bathroom. With a shriek, I call out to Shawn who sprints into our master bathroom. Out of breath, he nods toward me and I throw my arms around his neck.

"It's here! The lupron bleed is here!!!"

Shawn laughs and gives me a bear hug. Once again, this journey has done a complete three-sixty and my emotions have raged from one extreme to the other. Tears return, falling down my cheeks and I shake my head. If we can survive these treatments, then our relationship can withhold anything. We're better together and stronger than ever.

CHAPTER 17

A chill whips through the wind as I venture outside. I know I'm taking everything to extreme so when Dr. Valleroy told me to take it easy now that my ovaries are the size of golf balls in preparation for the egg retrieval, I am giving taking it easy a new meaning. What her words meant to me is that I should lie down in bed and not even lift a carton of juice. Shawn is being incredibly sweet and playing into my "take it easy" phase. Honestly, I think we're both doing a bit of pretending, acting as though I'm already pregnant because this could be the closest I'll ever be to it. If I'm honest, it was fun to lie around and be waited on hand and foot but now I'm just getting bored.

I tug the collar of my jacket up around my neck and wander to the side of the house where Shawn is untangling Christmas lights. He doesn't hear me walk up so I pick up a strand of lights and try to solve the mystery of how in the world lights that are put away so perfectly can wind up in such a crazy mess. Unlike my husband, the most patient man in the world, I only work on the puzzle for about twenty seconds before I start huffing and puffing and cursing under my breath.

"You're going to have to watch that sailor's mouth

you've got there when the baby gets here," Shawn teases me, kissing my cheek as he takes the lights out of my hand.

Shoving my hands in the pockets of my coat, I shake my head. "Don't say that, don't talk like you know there's a baby that's going to be here. You're going to jinx it!"

Shawn shakes his head with a laugh. "Babe, lighten up. Whatever I do or don't say won't determine our future. We're not living our life based off what the Magic 8 Ball predicts."

I bite my bottom lip and look away. If Shawn knows me at all, he knows I've already asked the Magic 8 ball more than once if this IVF will work or not. It's my guilty pleasure... when things work in my favor. When they don't, I allow it to get me more upset than it should.

Not even looking in my direction, Shawn comments, "I saw you downloaded the app." He glances over his shoulder at me with a smirk. "Just because you threw away that 8 Ball you had from junior high doesn't mean you haven't let go of it."

Giggling like a middle school girl with her Magic 8 Ball, I walk to Shawn and hug him from behind. "I can't help it. You know how much I hate to have zero control of a situation so this lets me pretend like I have a little bit of knowledge of what's going to happen."

Shawn rests his hand on top of mine. "That's fine, Jules, we all do what we gotta do, but don't let it get you upset. Now, tell me what you think I should do with these lights."

"The exact same thing you did last year! Some little girl and her mother are depending on us to brighten their day. They gave us fifty thousand dollars, Shawn, we can't let them down!"

Not a day goes by that I don't think of that little girl and her mother. I want to find them, I want to pay it forward, or back. I honestly just want them to know how grateful we are for what they did for us. We had no idea how we impacted them and they have no idea the gift they've given us. Even if the IVF doesn't work, Shawn and I both have been changed by winning that money and not in one of those T.V. documentary where winners end up gambling away all their money. It's made us both realize how it's the smallest things that can make the biggest significance to someone else. Still, I always wonder what kind of hardships that mom was referencing when she mentioned life had been rough lately.

"Okay, okay, I got it! Same blue and purple lights on the tree, manager scene, and one candle in the window. Can you handle the candle?"

Taking a deep breath, trying to relieve the weight of the pressure I just placed on both of us, I nod. Shawn smiles and drops the lights in his hand. He wraps his arms around me and kisses me forcefully. I get lost in the kiss, forgetting about the worries of perfect Christmas lights, fertility medications, and what life will be like without a child. This is why I love Shawn and why he's the perfect man to tame me and my wild ideas.

"Good. Now, go light that candle and rest up so that baby of ours can grow, grow, grow."

I narrow my eyes and he laughs, giving me a quick peck and waving me toward the door. Despite my glaring eyes, I smile as I walk back to the house and my mind darts to a place that I rarely let it go. I'm picturing a few years down the road with our child outside with Shawn, untangling the lights and shouting with excitement as one strand unravels after another. I bring them both a cup of hot chocolate and we have one of those Hallmark, picture perfect moments. Sometimes it's fun to let my mind wander but I know it's a dangerous place to venture.

Opening the door to the house, the warmth envelopes me and I quickly shed my coat. I didn't realize it was so cold outside until I came back in. I can at least make half of my fantasy come true. Turning on a burner, I put some milk in a pan to simmer while I pull out the rest of the ingredients to make hot chocolate, it might only be for two this year, but who knows what next year will entail? My mind quickly drifts, fantasizing about how many eggs we might retrieve and if we might end up with twins or even triplets! I laugh as I stir the hot chocolate, thankful that we haven't spent too much of our lottery earnings in case we have three babies at once.

My phone interrupts my day dream. With my free hand, I look at the screen and immediately my stomach drops as I recognize the number. Taking a deep breath, I hit 'accept' and put the phone to my ear. I wait a few seconds before saying "hello."

"Hi, is this Julie Hampton?"

"Hi, Mary, it's me," I greet Dr. Valleroy's nurse, dreading whatever it is she has to say.

"Hey, hon. Dr. Valleroy looked at your ultrasound from today and things look really good. You've got eight follicles on each side, ranging from 17-20 which is excellent."

I nod, a lump in my throat forbidding me from any type of response. I feel like every time I get a phone call from Dr. V's office, it's good news followed by bad news so I'm just waiting for the other shoe to drop.

"So based off your number's, we're going to schedule you for your egg retrieval on Sunday."

My heart drops to my stomach and I finally am able to mutter, "Wh-what? Sunday?"

"Yes, ma'am. You'll administer the HCG shot tonight at 7:30 on the dot then tomorrow you'll get a day of rest, no meds. Spend tomorrow resting up then report to the office Sunday morning at seven with a full bladder."

"O... okay," I mumble still in a daze.

"Julie?"

"Yeah?"

"This is a good thing, hon. I know you've been through a lot but things are looking great. We'll see you Sunday."

The phone call ends and I set my phone back on the counter. I didn't even realize I was still stirring the contents of the boiling pan as my mind was trying to comprehend everything Mary was telling me. This is it, the moment we've been waiting for and suddenly, I'm more scared than anything in my life. It's ridiculous, totally ridiculous, because I've been here before, in this exact situation and I know what to expect. I know why I'm freaking out but I don't want to admit it.

My brain on autopilot, I pour a mug of hot chocolate and walk back outside, forgetting about my coat. Like a waitress that's worked a double shift, I mindlessly hand Shawn the cup. He takes it and kisses my cheek.

"Thanks, babe, now get inside, it's freezing out here!"

"Sunday," I whisper.

Shawn looks at me, holding the mug to his lips but refraining from taking a drink. "Sunday what?"

"Sunday is egg retrieval day. HCG tonight at 7:30," I answer like a robot, still in shock that the day we've worked so hard for is now just right around the corner.

"Woohoo!" Shawn cheers, kissing me after he does. "That's great... so what's wrong?" He frowns. "Did the Magic 8 Ball tell you something else?"

His comment snaps me out of my trance and I frown. "Ha ha, very funny."

Shawn smiles. "There you are. Now, what's freaking you out?"

I shrug and shake my head. "I don't know... I guess just knowing what's happened in the past doesn't make me very hopeful."

Shawn puts his arm around me and squeezes my shoulders. "No more talk about the past. I'm done with everything here so let me put up the empty tubs then I'll come in and take care of you until it's shot time."

I nod, forcing a smile to my face. Looking around, I inspect Shawn's handiwork, ready to compliment him until my eyes land on the manager scene. I grab his hand and squeeze tightly while pointing with the other at Mary and Joseph.

"Wh-where is Jesus?"

Shawn gets that deer caught in the headlights look and moves his hand to the small of my back, trying to guide me inside. "I was just going to wait until later when it got dark to put Him out."

I shrug away from him, walking over to the tubs and throwing off lid after lid. "Show Him to me, Shawn, show me baby Jesus."

Shawn grabs both my arms, pulling me to stand up straight. I sound like a crazy person and I know it. In this moment, it doesn't matter what the Magic 8 Ball says or doesn't say, if baby Jesus is missing, this has got to be a bad, bad sign.

CHAPTER 18

My head is foggy and my eyes feel like they weigh a million pounds. I concentrate, focusing on opening just one eyelid so I can see who the voices around me are coming from. There's a steady beep from a machine and the people around me are speaking in medical jargon that might as well be a foreign language. I've been through this so I know what to expect but it still doesn't stop the slight panic from setting in after all my effort can't even get me to open one eye.

"Where's Shawn? Is my husband here?" I try to ask but my voice barely comes out as a whisper. My throat is so dry and my stomach growls from hunger since I couldn't eat anything after midnight which was almost eight hours ago now.

"Yes, Julie, Shawn is here. He'll be back to see you in a just a few minutes."

Hearing the familiar voice of Dr. Valleroy's nurse, Mary, I smile and start to relax. My eyes are still too heavy to open but I'm not freaking out like I was before. In only a matter of minutes, Shawn will be back here holding my hand and all will be right in the world again.

In the distance, I hear Dr. Valleroy's voice and I lean

toward where the sound is coming from, straining to hear what she's saying. Wishing she'd speak up, I interrupt her and whoever she's talking to.

"What did you say? How many eggs did you get?" I ask, one eyelid slightly cracked so I can see her.

"I believe we got thirteen."

I close my eyes and smile. "Thirteen... that's my birthday."

Warmth envelopes my hand and my smile gets even bigger. I don't have to open my eyes to know Shawn is beside me, holding my hand. His other hand pats my leg and he whispers softly in my ear.

"You did good, baby, you did real good."

My eyelids flutter, trying to open so I can see my supportive husband. His bright smile and dark eyes stare back at me and tears spring free, running down my cheeks. Shawn reaches over and wipes them away without saying a word.

"Well, Julie, looks like we're going to have to change your birthday. We got sixteen eggs. Every follicle you had, we were able to harvest. Now, not all of them were mature, but it's amazing that we were able to get all of them."

Shawn and I look at each other and we both start to laugh. This is the first time we've gotten every, single follicle and the most we've *ever* gotten. Baby Jesus may be missing from our front lawn but this egg retrieval seems to be some kind of Christmas miracle. Dr. Valleroy and her nurse tell us what comes next although we're already pros at this procedure. About an hour later, Shawn has me buckled in the front seat of his car and he's driving us home.

"Sixteen eggs... wow," he says, shaking his head in disbelief.

I laugh, grabbing my ovaries as I do, still sore from the procedure. "That's insane, isn't it?"

"What if every single egg got fertilized?"

I shake my head and smile, trying not to laugh. "Um, I may want to get pregnant but I don't want to be pregnant sixteen times."

Shawn reaches over and takes my hand. "Pretend with me. Let's picture our children and their futures." I frown and without even looking in my direction, Shawn squeezes my hand. "Don't do that, just relax and play along."

I sigh, knowing he's only trying to help and remembering how much I enjoyed pretending the other night, too. Shawn glances over out of the corner of his eye and smiles, knowing I'm on board now.

"Okay. Of course, our firstborn will be a boy. Since we're having sixteen kids, we might as well name our oldest son, Shawn Junior."

"Well, if we do that, then the oldest girl should be Julie Junior."

Shawn nods, his smile growing. "Yeah, I like that. Shawn Junior and Julie Junior."

I shake my head, already knowing what I want to name both a boy and a girl. Shawn stops at a redlight and looks over at me.

"Shawn Junior will be a first draft pick for the Cardinals, first base."

Smiling, I pat Shawn's hand that's on top of mine. "I like that. Free tickets for life for his parents, right?"

"Of course! It'll be like we won the lottery again if we get that."

My smile shrinks and I stare out the window. "Shawn, don't you ever wonder about that mom and daughter that left the ticket on our door?"

"I say a prayer for them every night, that their rough times are over and replaced with happy moments."

Quickly, I spin my head, looking in his direction. "You do? You pray for them? I didn't know you prayed every night."

Shawn smiles. "When I hold you at night, waiting for you to fall asleep, I pray in my head for everyone who needs help. Then I thank God for everything I'm grateful for, I like for it to be the last thing I think about each night, all the good in our lives."

I stare at him, in complete awe. He squeezes my hand and smiles.

"God is good, Jules. He'll take care of us, He knows what we can handle and what makes us stronger."

***

Numbers. Statistics. Odds. I strongly believe these could all be synonyms for fertility treatments. I'm still trying to wrap my mind around the numbers that Dr. Valleroy called with a couple days ago. Six eggs retrieved, four were too immature, twelve were fertilized, and we have eight embryos. Eight… eight… *eight!* The most we've ever had in a previous cycle has been four so we've doubled our chances this time! Yet, here we are still having proven Dr. Valleroy's facts, everything is fifty-fifty as in fifty percent of our eggs were fertilized. If we're talking facts and statistics, that means we'll end up with four embryos, transfer two, and hopefully get one baby. One, teeny, tiny embryo that will grow into a child of our own, that's all I want, just a fifty-fifty chance to be a parent.

Fun fact… the odds of winning fifty thousand dollars are one in thirty-two million, *thirty-two!* Don't ask me how but somehow, we beat those odds. We won fifty thousand dollars and now, we're taking the risk and betting twenty-thousand of it for a fifty-fifty chance. If I were a gambler, I'd think the odds were good but we've been down this road and lost before so it's difficult to get my hopes up.

"You okay?" Shawn asks from the driver's seat as we cruise along the highway.

I look away from where I was gazing at the passing buildings and shrug. I'm not about to nod and lie to my husband on what is going to be the most important day of our lives up until this point. My bladder, filled to the brim, pushes on my nervous stomach and I want to throw up, not so much physically but emotionally. Today is the day, we're doing a three-day transfer, the wait is over yet it's starting all over again at the same time. I've injected myself thirty-seven different times with four different kinds of drugs and that's the easy part. After today comes the hardest part of the entire procedure... the dreaded two week wait.

My phone rings, interrupting my thoughts and I hit accept immediately. Even though it shows up as an unknown number, I know it's Dr. Valleroy's office calling before I even answer. My heart beats wildly, afraid of the unknown they're about to tell me.

"Hey, Julie, it's Mary from Dr. Valleroy's office," she says on autopilot. I've heard the greeting before, I know exactly who she is, yet she still introduces herself like that every time. Like everything else in my world, I always wonder how they go about their day to day lives, going home to their families every night with the knowledge of how much heartache goes through their office every day. Luckily, Mary doesn't wait for me to respond before getting to the point.

"Everything looks good for the transfer so don't worry about that." I smile when she pauses because Mary understands me well enough to know exactly where my mind is. "You've got five great looking embryos this morning so we wanted to confirm how many you wanted to transfer."

A mix of disappointment and excitement slaps me in the face. Disappointment that our eight are now five and excitement of five potential babies. I glance over at Shawn, already knowing the answer to this question. Despite only a few days earlier when we were both pretending each of the eggs they'd retrieved was an actually child of ours, we both know there's no way we could handle being outnumbered by kids that much.

"Two. We'd like to transfer two."

"Perfect. We'll see you in a few minutes!"

The line goes blank and I stare at my phone, my eyes welling up with tears. Shawn reaches over and squeezes my leg. When I look up at him, silent tears fall down my cheeks.

"Julie, what's wrong? This is what we've been working for."

"Five. We have five embryos." This isn't why I'm upset but it's a good cover.

"Five is fantastic!" Shawn looks over at me and frowns. "Julie, we've got to be positive. This is the best cycle we've ever had. Our numbers for everything have been heads about the rest. Do I need to remind you about the last time we were headed for a transfer and we arrived to find out *none* of the embryos had survived?"

I shake my head, feeling like an idiot for why I'm so upset. Wiping at my eyes, I take a deep breath, trying to control my tears as I begin to explain the secret emotions that I've felt with every cycle we've ever done.

"I know, Shawn. I get it, I really do. This cycle is going awesome but..." I shake my head, fighting off another herd of tears ready to rain down my face. "With the start of every treatment, there's so much hope and excitement that this could be it, that things could work out this time. There's so much work that goes with all of this, the shots, the monitoring, making sure everything is just right for the egg retrieval. We had the egg retrieval and it went great. Then that small window between that and today, those three days were a break for me. There was no more pressure on me to produce eggs or to grow those embryos. It was just our embryos sitting in the lab, growing and multiplying and doing their thing and all I had to do was relax and wait."

I laugh at the word 'wait.' "For once, waiting wasn't a bad thing! It was promising and it wasn't all resting on my shoulders. So yes, Shawn, the transfer is exciting because if only for a few seconds, there will be two live babies inside me, but then the pressure is on... on me. You've done your part, the doctors have done theirs, and now it's up to me to keep these embryos alive and growing until they are little people in our arms."

I don't stop the tears, I let them fall freely knowing this is a great stress reliever for me. I've felt this way every, single cycle but I've been too afraid to say anything to anyone, even Shawn. A few minutes later, Shawn pulls into the parking lot and turns the car off. He squeezes my hand and runs his finger down my cheek. Taking short breaths, I try to regain my composure so we can go inside and get things rolling. Instead of trying to console me or tell me I'm crazy, Shawn kisses me softly and whispers the only words that could make me feel better in this moment.

"I have no doubt that our embryos are going to the best place possible, Momma."

CHAPTER 19

If I am pregnant, I pray that I never get put on bed rest. The last week and a half I feel like I've been nothing but a lazy blob. I might have taken it a bit extreme when Dr. Valleroy told me to take it easy and stay off my feet again. I unload the dishwasher in waves and haven't cooked since before the embryo transfer. I'm scared that if I stand on my feet too long, the babies might fall out. I know it's a ridiculous thought but when I've done nothing except watch Law & Order all day, my mind has thought of every possible scenario. One of the side effects that I'd forgotten about was the lovely constipation. It's bad enough to be stopped up but then being too afraid to push too hard when I'm on the toilet has made this almost unbearable.

At this point, I'm done Googling, researching, reading other blogs, etc… To be completely honest, I'm totally over it. I don't want to think about infertility treatments, talk about them, tell my story, read about them, or anything else remotely related. I just want this dreaded two week wait to be over so I can move on with my life, no matter what the outcome may be. On a positive note, the lab called and the three embryos we didn't transfer made it to freeze. It's encouraging that the babies continued to grow in a petri dish so hopefully they're doing the same thing inside my body. Not to mention, we have three totsicles to transfer at a later date although I'm not sure I can mentally go through this whole process one more time.

Between overanalyzing every little thing my body does, I have decided that we should take up stock in toilet paper. Every time I use the restroom, I wipe once, inspect, wipe again, inspect, wipe a third time, then yell at Shawn to come and inspect. It's ridiculous, I know, because even if there were anything on the toilet paper, it could be anything from spotting to miscarrying to implantation bleeding so it's really kind of pointless to even look. I'm only at day six of fourteen and I'm about to drive myself mad.

Just as the "bom-ba" part of the Law & Order theme song starts, my phone rings. Gladly welcoming the break from my binge watching, I look at the screen, surprised to see that it's Shawn's cousin, Savannah calling. Muting the television, I slide the bar to answer the phone and hold it up to my ear.

"Hello?" I ask tentatively, not sure if Savannah really meant to call me or if it was a butt dial.

"Hey, girl! How 'ya feeling?"

Narrowing my eyebrows, I'm confused at the intent of her question since we haven't told either of our families that we're currently in the process of another treatment.

"Um, good. You?"

Savannah laughs on her end of the phone. "Shawn told me what's up with you two, you don't have to hide it."

My face flushes red even though no one can see me and I stammer, "Wh-who else did he tell?"

"No worries, he only told me. I was asking about you the other day and he told me what was going on so I wanted to call and get your perspective on it because you know how men are."

Laughing quietly because I know exactly what she's talking about, I relax a little. "Yeah, I know how he can be."

"Honey, they're all like that, not just yours. So, tell me what's up? How are you feeling?"

Now, even though I said I was over talking about it, I still jump at the chance to discuss how I'm feeling. I don't know, I've always been like that. When something's bothering me, I feel like a good case of word vomit will at least let me vent my feelings and I could possibly feel a bit better.

"I'm feeling completely normal. My boobs aren't sore. I had some cramping the first few days, now nothing. No morning sickness, zilch, nada, nothing!"

"Whoa, girl, calm down. You're what? Three weeks pregnant or something like that? Some women are still recovering from the hangover they're carrying around from the night they conceived. It's perfectly normal to not 'feel' anything."

I bite my bottom lip, refraining from reciting any facts I've read over the last week. "I'm going to buy stock in toilet paper and I'm afraid if I am pregnant, my baby might come out as a serial killer because I've watched so much Law & Order."

In that contagious laughter of hers, Savannah doesn't hold back as she giggles at my statement. It doesn't take long for me to join her and not that much longer that tears are rolling down my cheeks and I'm finally feeling cramping but not from implantation. Once we've gotten ahold of ourselves a few minutes later, Savannah lets out a long sigh.

"Whew, woman, I haven't laughed that hard in a long time." She pauses and I can hear her grabbing a tissue out of a box. "Okay, it sounds to me that you've spent way too much time on that couch of yours. I'm coming over and taking you to dinner tonight. Get dressed up, look fabulous, and prepare to get your mind off things for awhile. Got it?"

I'm not sure why she asks "got it?" because she's already hung up the phone before I can even answer. Sighing, I stare at the all capital letters of Law & Order that are frozen on the television screen. I smile because Savannah is right, I need a distraction and I'm sure with her, my mind will be anywhere but on whether there's a baby in my belly or not.

***

This was a bad idea, a horrible idea. I should've picked where we could eat. It's bad enough we're eating at a Greek restaurant when I can't stand the taste of olives but even worse that every food on the menu is covered with feta cheese, an unpasteurized cheese that pregnant women aren't supposed to have. I find myself at a crossroads of my superstitions. Do I order like I'm pregnant and ask them to hold the feta or do I pretend like I'm not and take the risk?

"Whatcha thinking about over there?"

I look up from the menu like a child with their hand caught in the cookie jar. "Huh? Nothing, just trying to decide what to eat, that's all."

"Yeah, right." Savannah snaps her menu shut and narrows her eyes. "I told you, you're not supposed to think about the two week wait."

"I'm not, I'm just trying to figure out what to eat."

"If reading menus is that hard for you, I'd hate to see you reading *Fifty Shades of Grey*."

I smile and close the menu. "You're right. It's just, I don't know if I'm pregnant or not so I don't know what to order. Do I pretend like I don't even know it's an option and eat the feta cheese or am I risking my kid having three heads?"

Savannah's smile grows but she refrains from her boisterous laugh. "When I was pregnant, I drank a margarita the size of my head the day before I peed on a stick. So far, I don't think it's done any permanent damage to him."

I nod and set the menu on the table. "I know but you didn't have to go through all this, the limbo of am I or am I not. It's like my whole life is on hold right now, has been for the last decade."

Savannah sets her hand on top of mine and nods toward me. "Never put your life on hold, Julie. Whether you get pregnant through fertility treatments or a drunken one night stand, the world is so full of the unknown. What causes autism or peanut allergies? No one knows for sure and you can't live your life trying to solve the world's problems. I'm by far not the best mom in the world, I swear in front of my kids and laugh when they repeat after me. I feed them hot dogs and veggie straws and count that as a win for protein and vegetables. And some mornings, I pretend to still be sleeping when the baby wakes up so my husband will get him and I'll get a few extra minutes of sleep."

I laugh and wipe at the tear trying to sneak down my cheek. Savannah squeezes my hand in hers. With her free hand, she holds up her phone which has a photo of her son smiling as he stares at her.

"All I'm saying is that as a mom, we all screw up and the only thing that matters is that your kid knows you love them. After everything you and Shawn have done to get pregnant, there's no doubt in anyone's mind that you already love all your children more than anything else in the world. So what if you have a little feta cheese? You're still a woman, a human being so live a little and order the cheese."

Two tears fall down my face as I laugh at Savannah's words. "I know but what if I'm not pregnant? This is the only two weeks that I can pretend that I am and act like I'm all put out by the restrictions."

I quickly bite my bottom lip, having admitted out loud

for the first time how I've secretly felt with every cycle of IVF we've ever done. I want to be pregnant, not just to become a mother, but to have that experience, the no cheese, no alcohol, stay off your feet ordeal. I want to be able to exercise my original, primary purpose of being a woman.

Savannah grins as she pulls her hand back. "Well, I guarantee that there's at least one brand of ice cream on sale at the grocery store."

I stare at her, shocked at first by her words until I hear the tinkle of her laughter. In a matter of seconds, we're both laughing hysterically with the entire restaurant staring at us. I may not have been able to spend the entire evening, hell not even a few minutes, not thinking about the two week wait but I've got my mind in a better place than it was on the couch. Only a few more days...

CHAPTER 20

Sixty-two. Sixty-two times that my husband or myself have stuck a needle in my body in the last month and a half. I'm lying here in bed, recalling every prick and poke, and even though it's been over a course of almost forty-five days, I can remember each and every one of them. All the fears, concerns, and apprehension that went into each draw of the meds and each jab of the needle. Today, I'll get stuck one more time and find out if any of those shots were worth it.

Beside me, the sheets rustle and I feel Shawn's lips find the side of my face. "Morning, babe," he says casually, as though today isn't one of the biggest deciding factor of our lives.

Mumbling "morning" back, I roll to my side to face him. The sun still isn't up but I can see the outline of his body from the moon that is still hanging high in the sky. I may not be able to directly tell if his eyes are open but I can feel his eyes on mine and we stare blankly at each other for a good five minutes, both of us unsure what to say to start the day that may change our entire lives. Without a word, Shawn breaks our silence, leaning forward and kissing my lips softly.

"Today's going to be a good day, Julie, I just know it."

A smile takes over my lips as tears spring to my eyes. "Yeah?" I whisper, too afraid to say anything else.

Shawn rolls to his back, holding out his arm to which I promptly snuggle up against his chest, listening to his heartbeat. He runs his fingers through my hair and I can hear the smile in his voice when he speaks.

"Yeah. Think about it. We used the money we won from winning the lottery to do this cycle. Statistics show that the odds of winning fifty thousand dollars off a scratch-off ticket are one in a thirty-two million. It's a sign, Jules, the odds are with us. Today you're going to get good news."

I glance up at my husband in the dark. "Me? What about you? Aren't you getting good news, too?"

Shawn shakes his head and kisses my forehead. "I don't need to get good news. I already have it." He squeezes his strong arm around my torso then slides out of bed. "And since today is going to be a good day, I'm getting up early so I can get it started!"

Laughing, I stay in bed, feeling the opposite of Shawn and too afraid to let this day begin. I listen to him whistle as he gets dressed for the day, wishing I had his perspective of life. Then again, it's why we work, he's the yin and I'm the yang, we balance each other out. Today though, it doesn't matter. His whistling, his words of reassurance, they aren't helping, my stomach is still a ball of knots and I wish I had some kind of remote that I could just press the fast forward button on and get to the end of the day.

I close my eyes and bring my feet to my chest, curling up in the fetal position as I try to clear my mind of any and all thoughts. Right when my mind is almost completely empty, Shawn's large hand runs across my back, moving in a circular motion. The bed dips under his weight as he takes a seat and he leans his head down against mine.

"Baby, please relax. I know nothing will make you feel

better until you hear back from the doctor's office that there's a baby growing inside you but I feel good, the deck is stacked for us. We beat the odds of the lottery, we sure as hell can beat some fifty-fifty odds, don't you think?"

Opening my eyes, one single tear drop runs down my cheek. "What about the other odds that we've beat? One in eight couples deal with infertility, we're the one in eight. Did you know that one in almost ten thousand people die in a plane accident or that one in eleven million people have been attacked by a shark, those are bad odds that we don't want to win, but we could. Just because we beat the good odds *once*, doesn't mean every odd we'll beat will be in our favor."

Shawn pushes my hair out of my face and kisses me softly. "I just know, Jules, I just know. Call me after you leave the doctor's office and when you hear from them. I can be home in twenty minutes. I love you, baby."

He stands up and I nod. We've been here before and there's no point in us both being off work and a hot mess. Last time, I did nothing but whine and complain, making Shawn inspect the toilet paper every time I wiped until we got the call that the last treatment didn't work. This time, I told him to go to work so he could be distracted and I'd call him as soon as I found out anything. I'm beginning to think that wasn't my best idea but it's too late to beg him to stay at this point.

I watch him leave for the day and throw back the sheets, unable to delay any longer. In what is way too fast, I'm fully dressed and ready for the day. I'm wearing my lucky socks that I've worn to every appointment, my baby dust earrings that a lady I met online sent me, and the same shirt I wore when we won the lottery ticket. Shawn has me too wrapped up in this whole odds and luck thing right now but I'm just rolling with it.

Half an hour later, I'm walking into Dr. Valleroy's office and hitting the up button on the elevator, ready to get this over with. The doors open and I step inside, hitting the number three and taking a deep breath. The doors start to close but suddenly stop and slide back open. Much to my surprise, Dr. Valleroy steps in. We smile at each other awkwardly, neither of us quite sure what to say. Finally, she breaks the ice.

"So, Julie, how are you feeling?"

My mind races, afraid I might say the wrong thing. Very loud silence passes and then I finally nod and mutter, "Fine." The elevator pauses, preparing to open the door for our departure. Then, unlike I've ever seen her before, Dr. Valleroy turns to me with a genuine smile on her face. Her left hand covers her heart and her right hand lightly touches my forearm.

"I know today's the day, Julie, and I just want you to know that I hope the fifty is in your favor." She pats her hand against her chest. "Oh, I pray…" she starts then trails off as the doors open and she waltzes out of the elevator and into the office, not finishing her sentence.

In a daze, I stand there, dumbfounded by what just happened. Dr. Valleroy isn't like that. She's strong and professional. She's by the book and tells it like it is. She doesn't hide or beat around the bush, she—she prays… for me, for us, for our baby. Shaking my head as it hits me, I jump out of the elevator before the doors close on me and I move to another floor. Dr. Valleroy is just like each of us. She's human and she has emotions, she feels for us. She's the robot that she is because it hurts too much to be vested into all the lives of the patients she sees and the potential babies she might be able to give them. I've been misjudging her this entire time, she's not cold, she just cares too much.

"Come on, Julie, I'll get you in real quick before anyone else gets here," Mary says, snapping me out of my trance as I've barely stepped into the room. My mind still in awe of Dr. Valleroy, Mary dashes around me, directing me to take a seat as she gathers everything she needs to draw my blood. "So, have you cheated?"

Trying to push my thoughts of Dr. Valleroy aside, I shake my head, trying to clear my mind. Frowning, I repeat Mary's question. "Cheated? How so?"

"Pee on a stick!" she exclaims as though I should've known that.

I shake my head vigorously. "No, it didn't even cross my mind as an option."

Mary laughs as she presses the needle against my skin. "Some women are taking pregnancy tests the day of their transfer."

I brace myself as she breaks my skin and I let out the breath I was holding. "Even if I had thought of it, I wouldn't do it. If it's negative, I don't want to hear it twice in the same day, once is good enough."

Mary pulls out the needle, the vial of blood collected. She smiles at me as she places a piece of gauze against the bend of my elbow. "We're all thinking good, positive thoughts for you, Julie. I'll call you when we know something."

Immediately, my stomach sinks, already dreading the moment when I see that number pop up on my phone. I don't want to know the results, I want to continue living blissfully and pretending I might be pregnant. Once the phone call comes, the maybe will be confirmed one way or the other and my dream is either just beginning or turning into a nightmare…

***

It's almost four and Dr. Valleroy's office hasn't called. They close in thirty minutes and I haven't heard a single word from them. If they don't call today, I'm not sure I'll be able to last overnight to hear the results tomorrow. I've already had to talk myself out of going to buy a pregnancy test four times but if I don't hear from them by the time the office closes, I'm going to the grocery store and peeing on that stick in their bathroom.

I pick up my phone and look at it one more time but still, nothing. Squeezing my hands around it, I toss it on the couch and walk outside. My palms are so sweaty, I fear I might electrocute myself. Is it bad that I looked up the odds for that actually happening? The house is beginning to feel suffocating and I need some fresh air.

Stepping into the sunlight, I barely notice the chilly air as I close my eyes. I focus on the sun rays warming my skin, distracting me from what awaits from the phone call. Counting to ten, I breath in and out, forcing myself to relax and trying to remember breathing exercises I was taught back in high school. The temperature doesn't bother me until something cold touches my nose. Opening my eyes, I'm shocked to find snow falling around me. This wasn't in the forecast, in fact, there was a zero percent chance of rain. As if I just discovered what E equals, Shawn's words from this morning suddenly make sense. Luck is on our side and he's right, today is going to be a good day.

Running back inside, I race to the couch and pick up my phone. My chest rising and falling, I try to catch my breath as I read the screen. One missed call. This morning it was down to one little blood draw and right now, it's up to this final phone call. Slowly, I redial the number and brace myself for how my life is about to change...

EPILOGUE

Two Years Later

Back and forth, back and forth... I push the swing back and forth, feeling myself relax to the rhythm of the motion. The cool spring breeze blows through the air and I pull my jacket tighter around me as a shiver runs down my spine. Over a decade ago, I moved into this neighborhood single and childfree, witnessing this park evolve into the bright and colorful playground that it is today. I've spent many days watching children play on this exact playground, longing for my own child. I can't count the number of tears I've shed because of this playground, just thinking about all those memories makes my eyes sting. Taking a moment to push away the potential tears, the child I'm pushing jumps off the swing, running at full sprint to another part of the playground.

"Where do they get their energy?"

Knowing the tears are safely at bay, I turn to the woman beside me. She is pushing a toddler in the baby swing, a smile on both of their faces. The child is waving her hands, cooing happily as she sways with the rhythm of the swing.

"I wish I knew, I could use some of it."

She nods. "Me, too, but only because this one keeps me up to all hours of the night. I try telling her that sleep is good but she insists on the lifestyle of a night owl."

"Yeah, I remember that age. I miss how sweet and cuddly mine was but man, I sure love my sleep." We both laugh then I motion toward the child in the swing. "Is she your only one?"

The lady's smile diminishes and she nods. "Yeah."

"Think you'll have any more?" I ask although I hate that question.

She lets out a long sigh and shakes her head. "No. It took us a long time to have this one."

I smile, knowing exactly what she means and using it as my segway to another topic. "Been there and done that. She's my little IVF miracle." I point across the playground to the blonde, curly haired six-year-old hanging upside down from the monkey bars.

That familiar smile, the one that lets me know we're part of the same tribe, springs to her face. "Same here! Three IVFs here…"

"Wow, three? I guess we were lucky. I only did one fresh cycle then got pregnant with her from a FET."

My infertility buddy nods. "Yeah, we did three fresh cycles, three of our embryos made it to freeze but didn't survive the thaw."

Knowing 'I'm sorry' won't mean anything, I skip it and take a deep breath. "Fertility treatments aren't for the weak. It's so hard on everyone involved, physically, emotionally, financially. You have to have a strong relationship to survive, no matter what the outcome is."

"That's the truth! We were out of money then by some fate, someone left a lottery ticket on our door and we won enough to pay for one more cycle. I had made up my mind that this was the final cycle, it was either going to work or not." She stops the swing and picks up her daughter. "I'm grateful that it worked."

My heart speeds up and my stomach drops but I try to hide my emotion. "Wow, someone just left a lottery ticket on your door? Did you know them?"

She kisses her child's cheek and shakes her head. "Nope, a total stranger or as I like to call her, our guardian angel."

My mind races, trying to digest this information. Like the gymnast that she is, my daughter comes cartwheeling up to us, stopping directly in front of me. She turns to the lady and her toddler, pausing to say "ah" then looks up at the lady.

"What's your baby's name?" my daughter asks, never one to meet a stranger.

"Jaden. What's yours?"

"Summer." Summer takes the baby's hand and wiggles it. "Hi there, Jaden!"

I smile at Jaden's mom and nod toward my daughter. "She loves babies, I think all only children do. You know it would be a different story though if they had a sibling."

She laughs and nods. "I can only imagine. I'm Julie, I live down the road."

"Nice to meet you, Julie. I'm Melissa, we live right there. In fact, that's our black lab barking at us to come home."

"Mom, look at her eyes! They're so pretty!" Summer yells at me as though I'm on the opposite side of the playground and not standing right beside her.

I glance down at Jaden's pristine blue eyes that contrast beautifully with her caramel skin. "They are pretty." I look over at Julie's dark eyes. "Does she get those eyes from her dad?"

Julie shakes her head, laughing. "Nope, recessive genes from our grandmothers."

"Ms. Julie, can you and Jaden come to the park with us again?" Summer asks, as though there's never anyone here to play with.

Julie smiles and pats Summer's shoulder. "Absolutely.

Her daddy is in Cooperstown at the Baseball Hall of Fame so we'll be here a lot this week."

Summer squeals in excitement and hugs her legs.

"Do you know that house with the big, giant evergreen tree in the front yard?"

My daughter's eyes light up and before I can stop her, she blurts out, "Yes! You have the best Christmas lights in the neighborhood. My mommy and I left you a card on your door at Christmas when I was three."

The color drains from Julie's face as she gasps. Quickly, I reach out for Jaden in case she faints. Julie passes her child to me and grabs onto the pole of the swing set to catch her balance.

"You... you..."

I nod, not sure what else to say or do other than bounce this happy baby up and down while her mother tries to comprehend the truth my daughter just revealed. My face burns a neon red while Julie just stares at me and Summer runs back to the monkey bars.

Still dumbfounded, Julie shakes her head and mutters, "W-why?"

Looking around to make sure my daughter is out of earshot, I begin to explain. "Three years ago, I was going through the hardest time of my life. I needed something, anything positive to give me faith that despite my divorce and losing time with my girl, the girl that I'd hoped, prayed, and fought for, that the world would still keep turning and all would eventually be right in the world. Driving through our neighborhood, when we'd only been awake for a few minutes, my heart heavy with more grief than I'd ever experienced during all our years of infertility, our early mornings were lit up by the glowing Christmas lights. I don't know how I thought of the idea but I decided we would leave thank you notes on our favorite houses with a lottery ticket. It was someway that we could pay back the favor. You brightened our days, distracted me from the dark times I was experiencing, and we just wanted to say thank you."

Tears fall freely down Julie's cheeks and she reaches out, wrapping her arms around me. Overcome by her emotions and my own, I cry as we embrace, her sweet, baby girl patting us both on the back. Then, my little girl, who is the most intuitive person I've ever met, joins our circle, hugging both Julie and my legs.

Pulling back, Julie looks directly at me and shakes her head. "Well… what are the odds?"

WHEN ONE CHAPTER ENDS,
ANOTHER BEGINS...

ABOUT THE AUTHOR

Photo by Water to Sky Photography

Lyssa Layne is first, and foremost, the proud momma to her precious daughter, AR. In addition to working full-time and being a mommy to AR, she is also an avid St. Louis Cardinals fan, a runner, blogger, and an infertility survivor.

Having watched one too many medical dramas and being inspired by author Rachelle Ayala, who introduced her to the world of indie writing, Lyssa decided to try her hand at writing a romance story. Her attempt turned into the Burning Lovesick series. You can find Lyssa's own interests throughout her stories although all stories are fictional.

Contact Her:
- Website: http://www.lyssalayne.com/
- Newsletter: http://eepurl.com/bq2JQn
- Facebook: https://www.facebook.com/lyssalayne
- Twitter: https://twitter.com/layne_lyssa
- Pinterest: http://www.pinterest.com/authorlyssalayn/
- Amazon: http://www.amazon.com/Lyssa-Layne/e/B00KP1Y5BY
- Goodreads: https://www.goodreads.com/author/show/8280977.Lyssa_Layne
- Barnes & Noble: http://www.barnesandnoble.com/c/lyssa-layne

OTHER BOOKS BY LYSSA LAYNE

The Right Pitch

Loved by the Linebacker

Fear of Striking Out

Another At Bat
Over the Fence

Until You Fall In Love

Everybody's After Love

My Favorite What If

Holding the Other

My Calling

Unfinished Business

Catch My Heart: A Valentine's Day Collection

Love & Famiglia: The DiDominzio Novellas

Burning Lovesick Series:
Love is a Fire
Burst Into Flame
Love Can't Save You

BABY, MAYBE

Made in the USA
Lexington, KY
18 May 2017